The Maid of Cefn Ydfa

by

Isaac Craigfryn Hughes

JOHN JONES

The Maid of Cefn Ydfa

This edition copyright John Jones Cardiff Ltd.

Republished June 1979

ISBN 0 902375 55 5

Cover designed by Dragonfly Design, Cardiff

JOHN JONES CARDIFF LTD
41 Lochaber Street, Cardiff CF2 3LS

Printed by A. Wheaton and Co. Ltd., Exeter

INTRODUCTION.

Who in Wales, the " Land of Song," does not know something of the troubles and adversities of the " Fair Maid of Cefn Ydfa," and her unfortunate sweetheart, Will Hopkin the Bard ? Whilst the bases of the mountains of Gwalia are washed by the waves of its crystal rivers and whirling brooks, and as long as " Cymru, Cymro, and Cymraeg " exist, the sweet and heavenly-inspired " Gwenith Gwyn " will not be forgotten, or the circumstances under which it was written lost.

Some of the chief bards of Wales have immortalised the name of the broken-hearted maiden—the late " Mynyddog." the Rev. Dr. Pan Jones, and the Rev. W. Onllwyn Brace ; besides, a party of itinerant actors have constructed a drama founded upon the touching circumstances surrounding her history. I saw the performance once, and, although I do not attend such places in order to find fault, I must say, plainly and unequivocally, that it did not please me at all, because it treated the various characters, in my opinion, with great unfairness, and in a manner calculated to bring Welshmen of that period into contempt.

The Author of this novel does not claim infallibility. No, he knows his own failings too well, and the reader will not discover more imperfections in it than he has found himself. So, kind reader, pass them over and be merciful.

The story is intended to illustrate Welsh life and scenery, and the Author has done his best to depict them. It must be remembered that great changes have taken place in the moral, social, and religious conditions of the Welsh nation since the time of the " Maid of Cefn Ydfa." At that period, superstitious tales of corpse candles, apparitions, and fairies were popular amongst the masses. There was a ghost sitting on every stile, Gwyn ab Nudd visited the windows of the houses on Michaelmas Eve to beg potatoes and butter, and everybody was afraid to cross the threshold after sunset. In that period tales of ghosts and fairies, or, according to the language of Glamorgan, " Bendith y Mamau," and their kind, were the most popular pastimes of the people. But to-day the Sunday School and other educational means have, fortunately, driven such foolish things away, never to return. Whilst, however, describing the social condition of Wales at the beginning of the last century, these have to be taken into account, or an unfair and incorrect description of the different characters will be portrayed.

I feel that a further word is due with regard to the characters mentioned in the leading chapters of the work. They may appear, in name and character, like those seen in another novel known in South Wales ; but the careful and critical reader will observe that they differ materially in treatment. Several of the first chapters were written in 1873 with a view to a competition, but I was prevented from carrying out my purpose, and it was left half done. The object of making this explanation is to put a stop to the babbling of certain hypercritics that are to be met so often in Wales.

And now, I have only to wish god-speed to the story, and that the reader may enjoy it, and find in its pages some mental instruction.

THE AUTHOR.

Banks of the Taff,
    May 19, 1881.

THE MAID OF CEFN YDFA.

CHAPTER I.

THE VILLAGE INN.——THE TWO LOVERS.

THE first scene of our story takes place at the inn
of the rural village of Llangynwyd, which is known
by the pretentious name of "Royal Oak." There are
many pretty objects possessing no special merit, this inn
was one. It was a low thatched building, with whitewashed
walls, ivy-covered at one end. The floor was a mixture
of earth and lime, and the furniture consisted of a shelf and
dresser, with bright pewter plates upon it, which belonged
more to past ages than the present. In truth, everything
connected with the old inn, inside and out, was utterly un-
suited to the regal name it bore.

It was a stormy night in October at the beginning of the
last century ; and surrounding the old hearth of the inn,
and diverting themselves by the light of the wood fire, was
a small merry party. They were now and then joined by
the landlord, whose ready wit kept the company in a cheerful mood. He was a little man, and well suited for the discharge of the duties of his profession. He was brought up
in the school of hypocrisy, and had attained eminence
beyond that of the common run. When there was a funeral
he bent his head in an attitude of grief, and might be taken

for a saint, and the groans which escaped from him were enough to melt a heart of adamant. But on the occasion of a wedding the walls of the old inn would ring with his fun and laughter, The chief object of his life was to please the company in the house. He sometimes appeared very devout and put on a religious air; another time he would pretend to be an infidel, denying everything. He was like a weathercock, turning with every breeze.

Whilst the company were enjoying themselves the door opened and two young men, well known in the neighbourhood, entered. They ordered two cups of ale. The landlord obeyed at once, and the liquor was sparkling before their eyes in less than two minutes. One of them took his cup and did not remove it from his lips until it was drained. He then turned to his companion and said—

"Now, Jones, drink up that we may have another. It will put you in a better spirit to meet Ann."

A sarcastic smile passed over his countenance as he spoke.

"Where are you going to take Jones to-night, Jack?" asked one of the party.

"To Cefn Ydfa, of course," was the reply.

"What, in the name of fate, do you take him there for?"

"Don't you know that Jones intends to marry Ann? He has asked her mother's permission and obtained it, and to-night he is going to have a talk with Ann on the subject."

"Splendid, Jones. Putting the cart before the horse. Ha, ha!"

"Never mind, Jones is certain to secure his purpose. She will get wild when she sees his charming and angelic face. And, in addition to his personal charms, he has bought a new hat, specially made for himself. And besides, he has a handsome stick and a new pair of trousers ; so that between everything he is bound to succeed."

" Now, Jack, let us go, it is full time," said Jones, and off they went.

Jones was the only son of a small tradesman in the village, and was known as " Jones the Shop," whilst Jack obtained his livelihood by hauling wood from the forest on the backs of donkeys, and was known by the classical name of " Jack the Carrier." He was short of stature, ugly, and awkward in his movements—his head and feet forming the greater part of his personality. Jones was very deficient of sense, and his silly actions were the subjects of the laughter and contempt of his fellows. His head was covered by a hat twice the ordinary size, and more like a parasol than the usual head covering. His body was kept warm by a long-tailed blue coat, with brass buttons ; whilst his legs were covered by a pair of cashmere breeches, surmounted by pantaloons. In short, Jones was a gentleman, as far as dress was concerned—at least he thought so. Jack, his friend, was different ; plainly dressed, with a short pipe in his mouth, he was possessed of good sense and a lively imagination, and could do what he liked with Jones, whose dress that night was dictated by him.

After leaving the inn they walked silently together, the first to speak being Jones, who said—

" I have a splendid story to tell Ann to-night. I have been preparing it all day, and written it on paper. I know the will admire it, for it is so excellent."

" You are certain to succeed. She will be doting about

you when she hears it, and I bet she will be your wife in less than three months."

" Do you really think so ?"

" It is as true as that twelve pence make a shilling," answered Jack.

When Jones heard it he jumped with delight, and had to kiss mother earth for his folly. By this time they had reached Cefn Ydfa, but to their disappointment the family had not gone to rest. Whilst waiting in the cowhouse Jones suddenly asked—

" Do you think something of Mary, the servant ?"

" Not much, or of any of Eve's daughters."

" Then I suppose you intend to remain a bachelor ?"

" It is too soon to settle that matter yet. But, taking everything into consideration, it would perhaps be the best thing for me."

" I am not of that opinion, Jack. If I succeed in securing Ann's hand I shall soon be a married man. She is an angel of a girl. I am wild to see her. Go and see if they have all gone to bed."

Jack went, and soon returned, saying that they had not.

" Let us go to the window and see if they are at supper. It is full time for them, I think."

Jack agreed, and as they approached the house the dog began to bark, which frightened Jones so much that he ran away as fast as he could, and in his haste he fell, the hard ground making a mark on his forehead to remind him of his folly.

" I have knocked out my brains," he cried to Jack.

" I don't believe it, for you are not blessed with much of that valuable commodity."

" Oh ! I am bleeding fearfully. I feel the blood trickling down my face.   I am afraid I shall bleed to death."

" Don't be such a fool, and make less noise.   Perhaps the loss of a little blood will do you good.   Doctors often bleed people in order to cool their bodies, and the loss of a little blood will do you no harm.   It may cool a little of your passion for Ann.   There, wipe your face, and come on to the window, and ask for admittance."

" But that brute of a dog."

" Are you really afraid then ? "

" Of course ;   he'll bite me."

" Don't let that frighten you.   Take a big stone in your hand, and if he attacks you hit him with it."

Jones obeyed, and followed Jack, at the same time care-fully watching the enemy that caused his disaster.   The dog, however, did not notice them, and they were soon by the window.   Jack gave the usual sign, and Mary came out and asked, " Who is there ? "

" I," answered Jack.

" Oh ! it is you Jack.   But who is that with you ? "

" Jones the Shop."

" What does he want ? "

" He wants to see your young mistress, for he has something important to tell her.   Where is she ? "

" In her bedroom.   Where else should she be this time of night ? "

" Go and tell her that Jones is here, and ask her to come to her window and speak to him.   He has nearly stupefied me by talking so much about her."

Mary went as requested, and her young mistress was soon at her window. When she made her appearance Jones rushed forward in the direction of the window, crying—

" Oh, my beautful Ann ! Oh, my fair angel ! How I love you ! "

" What are you coming about the place like a robber this time of night for ? "

" Oh, Ann, I do love you, and I wanted to have a talk with you, for I love you with all my heart. I have already asked your mother to let me have you for a wife, and I beg you to say when you will marry me. I am yearning to see that blessed day."

" What are you talking about, Jones ? Are you mad ? "

" No, I know well what I am about. I love you, my fair angel, and wish to have you for a wife. I have plenty of money. My father has two thousand pounds in the bank, beside what he has elsewhere ; and, as I am his only child, I shall have everything after him."

" But there is something else besides money before talking about marriage. Without affection, the one for the other, riches will not make a happy home."

" But I love you, Ann."

Jones's store of speech was by this time quite exhausted. He could not for the life of him remember one sentence of the speech he had boasted to Jack that he had prepared. He stood dumb, pierced to the quick by the last words of Ann. Not a word could he say and the girl could scarcely refrain from laughing, seeing Jones with his hands in his pockets as mute as a gate post.   She was the first to break the silence by saying, " Is it become a Quakers' meeting, Jones ? And as I feel the cold I shall return to my chamber, Good night to you."

" Oh, don't go away, you will break my heart.   Stop a little, my beautiful girl."

But before the sentence had left his lips she had disappeared.   Jones then went in search of his friend, and found him sitting with Mary before the kitchen fire.

" Where are you going, Jones ? " asked Jack.

" Looking for you, that we may go home together."

" I am not going now.   You had better start, and I will overtake you by-and-bye."

Jones did not like the idea of returning alone, but after considering a little he turned his face towards home. Unfortunately, Jones was very superstitious.   He believed in all the traditions that prevailed at the time. He walked slowly and carefully, standing every three or four yards to listen. But there was nothing to hear or see. At last he reached a lonely and haunted spot called " Pwll Du," where goblins and witches were supposed to dwell.   Many were the tales told of their performances. One of them went to a farmhouse and asked the wife for a piece of cream cheese, which she refused.   The old witch turned away offended, telling the farmer's wife that she would be sorry for it some day.   The farmer possessed a valuable cow, about which he often boasted.   The cows arrived at the yard to be milked as the witch was leaving, and she went towards the cow and drew her hand across the grain of its coat, mumbling something that was unintelligible. The consequence was that the cow afterwards yielded water instead of milk. The incident caused much anxiety to the farmer and his wife. They looked upon it as an indication of something serious, and were induced at last to consult a conjuror. The farmer waited upon the wise man, who, after obtaining all the information he could, said that the animal was bewitched, and inquired carefully if any suspicious person had been seen about the farm. The farmer replied that he had not seen anybody, and the conjuror said he could not help him. He returned home with a heavy heart, and, relating to his wife the particulars of the interview, the wife remembered the incident of the old women and the cheese, and told her husband of it. The farmer went early next morning to the conjuror, and told him the story. " She was a witch," said the conjuror, " and you must send for her to undo the witchcraft." The farmer paid the conjuror his fee and went home. Early next morning he sent for the witch, who, after going through certain cabalistic ceremonies, restored the milk to the cow.

As Jones reached the Black Pool he remembered that the witch lived there, as well as the story of the cow. The remains of her cot seemed to him to gnash their teeth at the wind, and his hair stood on end as he looked at it. He became so frightened that he started at the sound of his own footsteps. Nothing strange occurred as he passed the solitary and melancholy ruin, but as he approached the hill leading to the church he thought he heard the sound of something following him.   He stopped and listened for a minute or two, but heard nothing. Everything was still, and he thought that his imagination was misleading him ; but as he formed that opinion he heard the sound again, nearer than before.   Suddenly, without consulting flesh and blood, he ran as fast as his legs would carry him, and his hat, showing no disposition to follow its owner in his flight, left his empty skull. And yet the sound came nearer and nearer every second, and the fright had a serious effect upon his joints and nerves.   On his way there was a small wooden bridge over a brook, which was dangerous to cross on a dark night, for it had no hand rail, and in his haste, and totally inconsiderate of the danger, he rushed wildly on the bridge and found himself in a pool under it, and the first word he uttered, when he came to himself was, " Oh dear ! they have drowned me."

CHAPTER II.

A FEW days after the incidents in the previous chapter, a great storm of wind rose, accompanied by heavy rains, over the parish of Llangynwyd. Many houses suffered from its effects, among them the ancient palace of Cefn Ydfa. The following days, all the masons and thatchers of the neighbourhood were fully employed repairing the damages. Mrs. Thomas, of Cefn Ydfa, employed a young thatcher named William Hopkin to repair the roofs of the house and barn. He was known as " Will Hopkin, the Bard." He was a young man of good presence, and noted for his wit and ready answers. Besides, he was possessed of a sweet and musical voice, and the hills of the neighbourhood often echoed his early song when going to his work. One day, whilst working at Cefn Ydfa, he sang one of his favourite songs, and standing near was Ann, the daughter, listening. She was much delighted with the singing, and, when dinner time came, he was invited into the house, and asked to sing the song again, and the family were much delighted with the sweet voice of the young thatcher. That afternoon he happened to be at the bottom of the ladder over which he climbed to the top of the house, and opposite Ann's chamber, and she spent most of the afternoon in conversation with Will. She felt there was something in him different to other men, and his words touched the tender chords that were hid in her heart.

Will Hopkin singing one of his favourite songs at Cefn Ydfa.

PAGE 10.

I understand that you have been very lucky of late, Miss Thomas," said Will.

" I do not understand you, William," was the reply.

" Was not Jones the Shop here last Monday night ? "

" Oh, I understand what you refer to. Yes, the simple fellow was here. Dear me, I never saw such a thick-headed fool and simpleton in my life."

" Jones is a handsome young man, and a lady's man in the strictest sense of the term."

" Yes, when his head is covered with that ugly hat of his. He came here and said that he had asked my mother's permission for me to become his wife, and that she had consented, and that he had called upon me to name the day. Did you ever hear of such folly ? "

" It is no wonder at all. Jones, whatever he may be, has an eye for the beautiful, and I am not surprised that he should forget himself whilst contemplating your angelic face."

" That's enough. None of that flattery, which I do not deserve, Will."

" If any young woman deserves to be called an angel, you have as much a right to the compliment as any one."

" I do not believe it, and it would be of no advantage to me. Let the matter drop."

" You heard, I suppose, of the accident that befel him when returning home ? "

" Not a word. Did anything happen to him ? "

" Yes, to be sure. When near the church he thought something was following him, and ran as fast as he could, and in his haste lost his valuable hat, and when he reached the bridge he jumped into the water."

" Don't say so ! Is it possible ? "

"As true as that you stand there. I saw his majesty this morning, and his face was ornamented with plasters, and his big head was covered with flannel. He looked under his ornaments a lively and blythe young man. If you could get his likeness taken as he is, it would be an important acquisition to the present age. He looks like an old man of 70."

"To be sure! I should like to see my unfortunate admirer, said Ann, laughing heartily. "But, William." she added, "let me hear the song of 'Shon y Saer ac Arch Mab y Gelli ? ' "

"You must excuse me, for I am not in the mood to sing it now, although I would, if possible, do anything to please you."

"Try, that's a good fellow ; I am so anxious to hear it."

At last, after much pressing, Will consented, but it is too long to repeat here. We'll give the facts upon which it is founded. It appears that the parish of Llangynwyd could not boast of its carpenters, there being only one, and all the work of the parish rested, consequently, upon him. He was often asked to make coffins for the dead. But as he was not a scholar, his method of recording the age was funny in the extreme. Instead of figures he used letters. For instance, for a young man of twenty, instead of 20 he would give XX. That slovenly habit of his gave offence to his customers, and the upshot was that a carpenter from another neighbourhood was induced to settle in the parish, who was, by the way, a scholar of the old fashion ; and, instead of using letters like Shon, put figures instead. The result was that the parishioners turned the stream of their custom towards the new carpenter. Shon hated the new-comer. But what was he to

do ? He knew that he was his superior as a skilled workman. Soon after the arrival of the new man, a youth
from the village was apprenticed to Shon, who boasted of
his scholarship ; and soon an opportunity was given him
to display his learning. Some families had continued to
employ Shon, and a son of one of them died at the age of
twenty-eight. Orders were sent to Shon to prepare a
coffin ; and the old fellow was proud of the opportunity
for his apprentice to show his learning. The coffin was
ready, and the name upon it, but not the age.

"Now, Dai, come here, my boy, and show what you
can do."

The apprentice obeyed, and asked what was the age of
the deceased.

"Twenty-eight," was the reply.

"Well, now, look here," said the apprentice, putting
down the figure seven. "That is seven, is it not ? "

"Yes," said Shon.

"Now, another seven will make fourteen," said he
whilst putting the figure alongside of the first.

"Yes, to be sure," said Shon.

"And another seven twenty-one."

"Quite right."

"And another seven twenty-eight."

"Splendid, my boy," exclaimed his master.

The coffin was taken to the house of the deceased's
parents. The time of the funeral arrived, and the corpse
was carried on the neighbour's shoulders to the church,
and from thence to the grave, before anybody had noticed
the inscription. Whilst standing by the grave when the
coffin was lowered, the old clergyman was struck with
surprise at seeing the four figures of seven. He wiped

his glasses, lest he was mistaken, and asked, " Where did you find this old patriarch ? "

" In this parish, sir," responded several voices.

" Seven thousand seven hundred and seventy-seven ! Older than Adam ! Where has he been hiding since the deluge ? " asked the son of Levi.

" In this parish, sir," was repeated. The clergyman then proceeded with the burial service.

For ages after this incident the greatest reflection that could be made upon the good people of Llangynwyd was to call them the people of the " old parish."

Will sang the song splendidly, imitating the various characters with such skill that his fair listener laughed till her sides were sore. As he finished, her mother was heard calling, and she left him, but not before her heart was wounded by Cupid's dart through the eyes of Will Hopkin.

Several days passed, and Ann spent much of her time in Will's company ; and the work was so much neglected that Mrs. Thomas' attention was drawn to it, and she remarked jocularly to Will that he would not win his porridge at the job if he did not take care.

" I never saw such a place," said Will, " I believe the old thatch has been bewitched."

" What makes you think so, Will ? "

" Because the slates I put on in the day time are taken off at night. I am inclined to think that the house is troubled like the palace of Gwrtheyrn long ago."

" No, Will, I hope none of the dragons hide underneath us."

" Well, I don't know about that, but there is something extraordinary here," said the young thatcher.

" I feel the cold, and must go in. Stay to supper to-night, and don't keep Ann out to gossip, lest she takes cold. She is young and tender."

Will promised to obey, although he felt reluctant to part with Ann, for he never felt so happy as when looking at her angelic face. The truth of it was Cupid had formed a knot which bound the poor thatcher and the rich heiress together. The night arrived, and when the members of the family gathered round the bright fire in the kitchen, Will Hopkin was the soul of the company, and gained constantly in the estimation of Ann. And when the time came to separate she accompanied him to the gate at the bottom of the field before the house, where they stood talking until the voice of Mrs. Thomas was heard calling, " Ann, come in." She went into the house, and Will wended his way homeward ; but his spirit followed the dear maid to Cefn Ydfa, who had made such a deep impression upon his youthful heart. He never reached home before with such a heavy load upon his heart. He felt that he was possessed by the angel of Cefn Ydfa, whilst considering the social distance that existed between them—she a rich heiress and he a poor workman. He tried to quell his troubled breast ; but notwithstanding all his efforts to curb his feelings, he experienced a strange void in his breast—his heart was gone.

CHAPTER III.

"ARE you ready ? " asked a well-known voice at
the door of the shop one evening.

" I shall be ready directly, I have only to put on
my new collar and get my stick."

" Don't be long about it, for it is late already."

The person thus addressed was our old friend of the
Shop, by Jack the Carrier, who was on his way to Cefn
Ydfa. Jones was soon ready, and both started on their
journey. Jones walked slowly because of a desirable
and pleasant (?) boil that had developed upon his right
thigh. Not many days had elapsed since nature had
graciously shown its interest in Jones by making this
addition to his house of clay. He related the occurrence
in so serious a manner as to excite the risible faculties of
his friend.

" You must have been a fool to have run over so dangerous a place on a dark night."

" But the ghost was at my heels. Oh ! Jack, to think
of that awful night makes my blood freeze in my veins."

" Don't be such a simpleton, that's a good fellow.
What ghost do you think was following you ? There
never were such things as ghosts and fairies."

" I know better, Jack. Do you remember how Twm
Tyhen was carried by a spirit to a cave, where there was
a bag of gold hidden, and how he was forced to carry it on

his shoulders to the bank of the river Llyfnwy, and throw it into the water, not daring to look back."

" Are you soft-headed enough to believe such nonsense ? "

" Yes, for I heard Twm tell the story himself, and he is well and hearty to-night, and would readily repeat it. Don't you believe it now ? "

" No : neither would I believe Twm further than I could see him. A bigger liar never was born."

" You are an infidel, Jack."

" And you are no better than a lunatic, to believe such follies."

" H'm ! Let us change the subject. What do you think of Ann now ? "

" The same as usual. She is a fair and lovely girl, and greatly blessed will he be who has her for a wife."

" He would be a lucky man : would he not, Jack ? "

" Particularly so."

" I hope that I shall be that fortunate individual."

" You stand a good chance for it."

" Yes, and I have a good story to tell her to-night."

" So."

" It is splendid enough to drive her out of her senses."

" Very likely, if it is like the author. Don't forget it."

" I have been all day committing it to memory. I will inform her how rich my father is, and that a new stock has arrived from Bristol, and that my father is going to take me to Bristol next Christmas to see the place ; and—"

" That's enough nonsense now. If you have not a better story than that to suit her taste it would be better for you to return home at once."

Jones said not a word, and they walked on silently until they reached the "Black Pool," when Jones tremblingly remarked, "Oh! Jack, if you knew the fright that possessed me when I passed through this lonely place! My hair stood on end whilst thinking of the old witch who lived here long ago. Oh! dear me!"

"I cannot but believe that you are doing your best to make a lunatic of yourself to-night. What is the matter with you? You are more childish in your conversation to-night than I have ever known you before."

"It is no reason that I am becoming insane because I am afraid whilst passing this old place. Remember what Will of the Lletty saw here a few months ago."

"Jones, for the sake of the Virgin and the Saints, don't bother me any more about ghosts and witches, otherwise I shall return, and leave you here alone."

They had by this time reached the field leading to Cefn Ydfa, when Jones imagined that he could hear strange and horrid noises, and fancied it was the roaring of the bull. He was terribly frightened, and would not move from the spot.

"Come on, and don't be such a simpleton," said Jack.

"I won't. I am afraid it will chase and overtake us. We shall be done for."

"It is scarcely necessary for you to be frightened at such a thing. You are blessed with such good limbs that it would be difficult for it to catch you."

"But this miserable boil on my thigh would prevent me running as fast as I otherwise could. I will not risk my life whatever may be the consequence."

"No, your life is too valuable! Greater loss has often happened, in London, before breakfast."

I will not risk crossing the field on any account."
And Jack was obliged to go back and go by the road,
which made the journey to Cefn Ydfa much longer. At
last. after long walking, they reached the yard, when the
dog—Jones's old enemy—began to bark.

"Here's that old devil beginning to-night again. I
would give you half a sovereign, Jack, for killing him.
He and I will never be friends."

"Do you think I would kill an innocent creature that
has done no harm to anyone ? " asked Jack, as he turned
towards the dog and spoke kindly to him—" Tango, my
good fellow, what is the matter with you ? Do they
annoy you, my friend ? " The dog wagged his tail, and
stopped barking. "That's the way to make friends with
the dog, and not by threatening him with a stone. Your
conduct towards the dog is like what it is to other beings,
whose affection you canont win."

Jones listened attentively to this severe lesson of Jack's
without uttering a word. When they approached the
house they found that the family had retired to rest.
Jack crept gently in the direction of the window, and
gave Mary a signal that he was there. He had not to
wait long before she opened the door. Jones went to
the window of Ann's room, and tapped the window.

"Who is there ? " demanded an authoritative voice
within.

"I am."

"Jones the Shop ? "

"Yes."

"My silly friend, go home. There is no one here who
wants to see you. Don't make yourself the subject of
ridicule and contempt to the whole neighbourhood."

" Oh ! Ann, your heartlessness kills me. Come to the window for a few minutes, for I have a matter of importance to put before you."

She obeyed, and as Jones saw her face he called out :—
" Oh ! my beautiful angel ! How greatly do I love you ! I should be willing to die for you to-morrow morning, if need be, my lovely dove."

" Hush, Jones. Don't be so weak-headed. A few minutes ago I was an angel ; now I am a dove. I do not believe that you know what you are talking about. It is full time to place you under the care of somebody."

" Oh, my dear Ann ; I love you so much ! I bought a new suit of clothes yesterday in order to appear worthily in your presence. Listen to me, and consider how deeply I love you."

" Jones, my good fellow, go home, before the moon set lest you should fall into the brook again, and be drowned, perhaps."

" If you refuse to become my wife I should care not if I were drowned, for my life would be nothing but pain and trouble."

" Be a man, Jones, and look out for a girl that would suit you better than me. I do not care for you, and could not be brought to like you."

" Is that your last answer ? "

" Yes," was the reply, and at the same time she closed the window and disappeared. Jones stood speechless, and as motionless as a statue. He did not seek his friend, but went straight home. He walked slowly, with bent head and taking no notice of anything—his disappointment being so great. He felt that the beautiful and flowery path he had pictured for himself was surrounded by thorns. The disappointment shadowed the future from his view. Whilst his mind was brooding over his condition, he heard a voice accosting him :—

' How are you, Jones ? "

" Who is there ? Oh, Dai, is it you ? I am not well at all. How are you ? "

" Very well, thank you. Where have you been to ? Cefn Ydfa ? "

" Yes, I have been there."

" Did you see Ann ? "

" Yes, I have been talking with her."

" What did she tell you. Did she promise to marry you ? "

" No ; the very opposite."

" I thought so. Do you know who is her favourite ? "

" Not I ."

" Will Hopkin, the Bard."

" What are you talking about ? Do you suppose that a young lady of the wealth of Miss Thomas would marry a poor thatcher ? "

" As certain as I am standing here ; and, unless something untoward happen, she will soon be his wife."

" I cannot believe it. The thing is impossible."

" You may do as you like, but you will soon find out that I am telling the truth. Whilst Will is allowed to talk with her there will be no chance for anybody else. I have heard also that Will is on the books of her mother."

" I must get him out of the way, or my efforts to win her will be unsuccessful."

" You may depend upon that."

" What would you advise me to do ? "

Dai drew closer towards Jones, and, speaking low and cautiously, they conversed for a long time. When they parted Jones's spirit revived, and he whistled cheerfully. Dai must have suggested something to help him to secure the hand of the heiress of Cefn Ydfa. What was it ?

CHAPTER IV.

ON one of the days following, whilst Jack the Carrier was pursuing his avocation, he met Will Hopkin. with his working tools on his shoulder.

" On the tramp again, is it ? "

" Yes, I am off again."

" Where to now ? "

" To Gelli Dawel."

" Within ten minutes' walk of Cefn Ydfa ? "

" You will, no doubt, have many an opportunity of meeting Ann."

" Why do you bother me about her ?   Do you suppose that a wealthy heiress like her would look at, to say nothing of favouring, a poor workman like me ?"

" Well, that is the talk between every two in the neighbourhood.   And I have lately had reason to believe it from a reliable source. Love despises social conditions."

" You know better, Jack.   Nothing of the kind has happened between Miss Thomas and me, and I can assure you that I have never made love to her, or even dreamt such a thing."

" I do not think that matters bear the same aspect in her mind.   She thinks much of you.   You can depend upon it."

" I cannot believe it. Consider the wealthy candidates for her hand."

" Who are they ? "

" There is the eldest son of the Plas."

" There is not the shadow of a foundation for the
rumour, for he is about being married to the eldest
daughter of the Glyn."

" Well, Mr. Jones the Shop, is another."

" Say the Fool of the Shop, and you would be nearer
the mark. No, he has been rejected, and the house forbidden to him."

" Were you with him when he was at Cefn Ydfa ? "

" Yes, I was fool enough to accompany him twice. I
never saw such a stupid dolt. He was enough to make
one giddy with his foolishness. The doctrine of courting
is a difficult one to unravel, and he is as ignorant of it as
Watt, the donkey, is of the movements of Jupiter. One
would think when seeing him in the society of the fair sex
that he is quite a ladies' man. He is like Andro, the donkey, with his eyes always full of winks, with the difference
that Andro uses another member to perform that important operation, namely his left ear."

" Well, let me hear some of his pranks."

" Well, to be brief, I happened to call at the shop one
day when his majesty was present. He began at once to
ask questions about Ann of Cefn Ydfa, and her mother,
&c., and if Ann had a sweetheart. I saw at once how the
wind was blowing, and answered that I knew of no one,
but that she was just the one to suit him. ' Do you think
so ? ' he asked seriously. I replied that I was serious.
He then asked me to accompany him to Cefn Ydfa that
night, handing me at the same time half a quarter of
tobacco. I promised to go with him, and gave him a few
hints how he should conduct himself, and to be properly

dressed for the occasion. At seven o'clock we started upon our journey. Jones had donned his best suit, and carried a stick in his right hand, with a blessed hat covering his empty pate. We turned into the Royal Oak, and, after refreshing ourselves, resumed our journey, and reached our destination in half an hour. I was almost stupefied with his silly nonsense, and the fool had written his love story for repetition to Ann. He was forced to kiss the ground twice because of jumping for joy. When we approached the house he was frightened by Tango, the dog, and I had much trouble to get him to pass that creature. I sent word to Ann by Mary the servant that a young gentleman wished to speak to her upon an important matter. I succeeded in getting her to come to the window. I went inside, and sat with Mary by the kitchen fire, under the belief that I should have to wait some time before Jones returned, but, as I am alive, he was back in a quarter of an hour, and asked me to accompany hm home. I refused, and he had to go alone ; and when he reached the hill leading to the church he thought that something was following him, and ran as fast as he could until he came to the old bridge, when, it appears, he attempted what he could do in the character of a gander, with a narrow escape from being drowned."

Will listened attentively to Jack's tale, and laughed heartily.

" I understand that he is a skilful lover," said Will.

" He is a skilful simpleton," rejoined Jack.

The two thereupon separated—Jack after his donkeys, and Will to his work. Will walked slowly, his head bending towards the ground. Only one thing occupied his mind constantly. The murmuring of the crystal rivulet, which meandered slowly through the meadow below, aided by the morning breeze, produced a strange impression upon his mind. He believed that the choir of the woodland were singing the praises of his beloved as they lifted their morning song to heaven. None but the experienced can realise the extent to which the mind travels when under the effects of the love fever. So it was with Will Hopkin. Everything appeared more beautiful that morning than ever before.

At last he reached the Gelly, but the same thing occupied his mind. The truth was the Maid of Cefn Ydfa had a deeper place in his affections than he had thought.

As the shell, taken from the seashore, speaks of the place whence it was taken, so the mind of the lover wanders after and discourses of the object of his affections, whatever may be the difficulties in the way.

The scattered thoughts of the young thatcher interfered with his work, and he was obliged every day to undo what he had done in order to put it right.

About sunset that day he noticed a young girl coming towards him. He recognised her at once as one of the female domestics of Cefn Ydfa. When near him, she beckoned him to approach her, and told him that her young mistress wished him to call at Cefn Ydfa that evening, and he hurried home to prepare for the visit. When he arrived the members of the family were gathered around a bright fire, whilst on a small table in one corner of the kitchen sat Robert, the tailor, diligently plying his needle. Robert was tall, thin, and muscular, and the hoar frost of time had touched his hair and beard. He was notorious for his superstition, even in that dark age,

and feared to cross the threshold after sunset, believing
every story, however absurd it was, about ghosts, corpse
candles, witches, and fairies.

The subject of conversation when Will entered was a
young man in the neighbourhood who was troubled wth
an evil spirit.

" Do you believe such a thing ? " asked Will of Robert.

" Of course.   Don't you ? "

' No, I cannot believe such absurd folly.   Do you believe that the spirits of the departed are at liberty to visit
the earth when they please ? "

" No, not likely," interposed Dai, the servant.

" No," answered Will, " it is unreasonable to believe
such a thing. The inhabitants of heaven do not desire to
leave it, and the inhabitants of the land of night are not
permitted ;   your   doctrine   is   opposed   to   reason   and
Scripture."

" Do you think that men are so presumptuous as to
speak what is untrue when they say that they are followed by spirits ? Why should they invent such lies ? "

" Speaking the truth is contrary to the nature of some
persons."

" I am sorry for you.   You are next door to being an
infidel," said the knight of the needle.

As he finished speaking, he screamed, and exclaimed,
" Oh God ! "

" What is the matter, Robert ? " everybody asked at
the same moment, and it was found that in the heat of the
discussion he had stuck the needle in his finger, leaving
half of it embedded in the flesh. When the company
realised what was the matter with the knight of the
needle, he was the subject of ridicule and laughter. The

dog and the cat seemed to enjoy the fun. Will went home after supper, and Ann, with Mary the servant, accompanied him part of the way. When about the middle of the field they met Jack the Carrier, and Mary joined him, leaving Ann and Will to themselves. Will saw in it an excellent opportunity to declare his feelings, which he did in trembling accents. Ann begged him not to trifle with her affections, but Will assured her that he gave expression to the sentiments of his heart.

" Do you really love me truly ? " she modestly asked.

" With all my heart," said the young thatcher, at the same time drawing her to his breast, and impressing fervent kisses upon her lips. This was their first meeting as lovers, and there, with only the moon and stars as witnesses, they swore everlasting fidelity to each other. An hour passed quickly, and Mrs. Thomas was heard calling her daughter, and in obedience Ann returned, but not before promising Will that he should see her next morning.

As Will was crossing one of the fields he thought he could see something moving slowly under the shadow of the fence, and after observing it carefully he came to the conclusion that it was a sheep. He was soon overtaken by Jack the Carrier, who was anxious to know what had passed between him and Ann. Will replied that nothing particular had passed between them.

" You are very foolish, and much to be blamed," remarked Jack.

" How can you say that ? "

" Beacuse you have fully won her affections.'

" I never proposed such a thing. I always consider that there is too great a distance between us socially to entertain such an idea for a moment."

" True love takes no note of social distinctions ; they are regarded, like gold and silver, as dross."

· " But she has not given any reason to suppose that she cares for me ; and if she does, she is wise in keeping it to herself."

" You must be a blind simpleton, and standing in your own light. Miss Thomas loves you—and loves you truly. Her love is no pretence, you may depend upon it ; and if you regard her conduct towards you in the light of friendship, you misjudge her grievously."

" I cannot believe you. It is impossible for such a thing to be."

" You may do as you like, but I know that I am right ; and now, good night," and whistling cheerfully, Jack went his way. Will was pleased that he had not satisfied Jack's curiosity, and felt his mind easy. He looked forward to the distant future when he and Ann would be married, and the sun of prosperity should brighten their path, and under such impressions he closed his eyes that night. But oh ! the future was shrouded by thick clouds of darkness, which obscured his view. He was building grand castles in the air, which were destined to crumble to dust and bury the builder in their ruins. The future had in store a number of bitter troubles and disappointments for the young thatcher, who was like one sowing the wind in order to reap the whirlwind ; and the enemy was already at work.

CHAPTER V.

EVERY village in Wales has its annual fair. It is looked forward to for months before it takes place. This is the happy time when servant boys and girls obtain their freedom and receive their wages; and if they do not like to remain where they are they have the opportunity of obtaining other places. Every child also looks forward to the fair, and counts the days and hours, and even the minutes between then and the day, when it expects to receive presents from friends and neighbours. The old practice was popular in Wales in the olden times, and, although it has largely disappeared, it is still held in honour in the agricultural districts. They are known as "hiring fairs." Early in the day servant men and maids who seek new places range themselves in rows waiting the farmers to come forward to hire them for the coming year The young women are blessed with aptness of speech, and relate the circumstances of the past year and the special incidents they have met with. Whilst talking their hands are not idle, but are busily engaged in knitting, the men standing in a row opposite.

The old town of Bridgend was once celebrated for its hiring fairs. Early in the day the farmers might be seen going to the fair, some driving their oxen and sheep, whilst their chief object was the hiring of servants for the coming year.

The family of Cefn Ydfa stood in need of an extra ser·
vant, and the night before Mrs. Thomas instructed her
daughter to look out for a suitable girl. Ann was delighted with the commission, and early next morning she
was seen going towards Bridgend on horseback. She was
not slow in reaching her destination. When she reached
the inn, where she put up the animal, whom should she
meet but Will Hopkin.

" What a wonderful and unexpected meeting," said
the young bard.

" In the name of the dear one, what has brought you
here, Will ? " asked Ann.

" Probably the same errand as brought you," responded Will.

Then they walked through the streets until they came
to a cross road, where they separated, having arranged to
meet again later in the day. Ann went in search of a servant maid, and soon being successful in her object, went
for a stroll about the town. Whilst looking at a shop
window she felt a gentle tap on her shoulder, and upon
turning round she saw to her astonishment and regret
that it was Jones the Shop. Without regarding the crowd
in the street, Jones shouted, " Oh, Ann, dear ! How
proud I am to see you. I have been searching for you all
over the town, and my efforts have been unsuccessful
until now."

Ann was dumbfounded, and did not know what to
say. After a while she asked—

" How came you to know that I was in the fair ? "

" Will of the Gelly told me that he saw you going, and
I prepared to follow as soon as I could. I could not
stop at home when I knew that you had gone to the fair."

" It would have answered your purpose better if you had stayed at home. I have told you more than once that I would have nothing to do with you, and I beg of you to leave me, for I have no wish to talk with you."

" Your refusal is certain to be my death. Do reconsider the matter, otherwise I shall lose my senses."

" I think, Jones, that nature has saved me that trouble," and she turned away with a smile of contempt playing upon her face.

Jones would have made a splendid subject for an artist to depict as a disappointed lover. If a thunderbolt had fallen he could not appear more frightened.

He stood mute and still, knowing not what to do. After a while he moved on and entered a public house, in which a harp was being played. He sat down for a short time, but nothing would ease his troubled mind, and he soon left. He walked up and down the street until his attention was attracted by the sound of a drum and other musical instruments, and going in the direction of the sound, he found that a show was going on. When the music ceased, the showman appeared on the platform, and dwelt upon the wonders exhibited inside. Among other things was a splendid picture of a battle between the British and the French, in which the former obtained a glorious victory. There was also a giant, whose body appeared like that of Esau, the son of Isaac, and the performance was to close with the exploits of Toby, the learned pig, who could tell how many days there were in the week, how many months in the year, and other interesting matters. The admission " was only one penny," as the showman said. Our old friend of the Shop made up his mind to go in, and was much delighted with the

picture of the battle, and with the giant. At last Toby
was introduced, who acquitted himself worthy of the
scholar of the pigsty. After informing the company
what day of the week and the month it was, his mistress
asked him to point out the youth who had lost his sweetheart at the fair. Toby went round, and stopped before
Jones the Shop. The mistress pointed to several young
men who stood near, and asked if this or that was the person, but Toby shook his head. At last she pointed the
rod at Jones the Shop, and Toby intimated that that was
the unfortunate individual. Everybody by this time was
looking at Jones. The mistress again asked Toby if he
was certain that the gentleman who wore the particular
hat was the one. Toby continued to intimate that he
was, and Jones became the subject of the laughter and
ridicule of the crowd. It was more than his nature could
stand, for his temper was already excited, and, full of fury
he attacked the woman, and would have throttled her if
the showman had not come to her rescue, and before five
minutes had elapsed our old friend of the Shop was lying
on his back outside, covered with blood and fearfully
maltreated, and tc crown all, he had lost his hat and stick
and was the possessor of a pair of black eyes. He remained unconscious for some time, and when he came to
himself he saw Ann of Cefn Ydfa coming towards him,
resting on the arm of Will Hopkin. They passed on, and
Jones thought that Will smiled contemptuously at him.
His madness had now reached its extreme point, and, as
he rose to his feet, he muttered, to himself, " He is the
cause of all this, and I'll have my revenge upon him if it
costs me my life," and away he went.

CHAPTER VI.

THREE WORTHY FRIENDS.

THAT night, under the shadow of a tree, in a seques-
tered place not far from Cefn Ydfa, there were
three men in earnest conversation. It was easy to
form an opinion, from their outward appearance and
rough language, that two of them belonged to the very
dregs of society. Every sentence of theirs was accompanied by foul oaths. The third person was better
dressed, and his language proved that he was superior to
his companions. It was a dark and disagreeable night.
There was not a star to be seen, and the wind moaned in
the branches of the trees. Now and again the silence was
broken by the dismal screeching of the owl in a hollow
tree lower down in the valley.

" Providence takes care of its children," said one of
the trio, smiling.

" Yes ; we could not have a better night if we had the
making of it ourselves."

" Now the time is short ; let us begin the business at
once. How much do you expect ? "

" You know that it is dangerous work ; and if it
should come to be known who did it heaven only knows
what would be our fate. We shall be hung like dogs.
What do you say, Dai ? "

" I leave the matter in your hands, and will agree with
your terms, and the payment."

" Well, taking everything into consideration, I do not think I shall be far wrong in asking ten guineas."

" Too much, Billy, my pocket will not afford it."

" Then you must be satisfied with your fate. Hush ! What is that ? "

" Some persons passing," whispered Dai.

" Be silent, or we are undone."

Just as the last sentence was uttered, a young man and young woman passed, talking merrily.

The youngest of the trio knew who they were, and he gnashed his teeth with rage. When the sound ceased in the distance, Dai said :—" It is they returning from the fair."

" Yes," observed the youngest, " if we agree, it is the last time for him to return with her from the fair, or any other place. Oh, that I could put an end to the life of the beast ! I should feel proud, even if it cost me my life."

" There is no need for that. If you only agree to the terms he will never be seen with her again, or anybody else."

' But I have told you before that your price is beyond my reach."

" What have you in your pocket now ? "

" I have only seven guineas in the wide world."

" It is too small a sum. We cannot undertake the dangerous work for that."

It was easy to see that the two friends were very anxious to get the money, and were almost ready to accept the seven guineas.

" See, Billy," said Dai, " What if we took the seven guineas to-night, and the remainder in a week ? "

" ' A bird in hand is worth two in the bush,' Dai.

" That is always my motto."

" That is all very well, but that was not your motto when the Gelly barn was burnt."

" Dai, hold thy peace in a moment, or this "—holding his clenched fist towards him—" shall help thee to go through the job," said Billy.

" Remember that I am not afraid of thee, and thou shalt find that thou hast met thy match. But this is not the way to do business. We had better take what Mr. Jones has to-night and the remainder in a week."

" Well, if we agree to that, who is to become Mr. Jones's security for the remainder ? "

" I will at once, if you are satisfied."

" Satisfied or not, remember that I shall come upon you like a knave when the time is up."

It was so arranged.

" Now, the next question is, where shall we put him ? "

" That is easy enough. You know the salmon pool," said Jones.

" Yes ; we know it well."

" Well, put him there. You will see that I have pre pared a coffin for him," observed Jones, spreading a sack before them, in which there had been flour.

" Excellent ! Ha, ha ! He will be in his new house before an hour is past."

" Hush ! " exclaimed Dai, rising to his feet frightened, " there is someone behind the bush." All were silent for a moment, and listening, but there was nothing in it.

" What do you think it was, Dai ? " said Billy.

" I thought I heard someone passing by the bush."

" For heaven's sake don't begin to dream now, but be wide awake until everything is over."

All was silent until something was heard a second time behind the bush. One would imagine, whilst hearing them talking when no enemy was near, that they were three heroes, and that fear was foreign to thm ; but when there was need of true courage they were not better than cowards. The sound behind the bush made their tongues cleave to the roofs of their mouths. Neither of them would venture out of his hiding place. But they had not to wait long, for the object of their fright bellowed until the sound reverberated through the valley.

"What fools we are," said Dai. "It is only one of the oxen of Cefn Ydfa. Now, Jones, my boy, go up and watch, and when you hear him coming let us know. Run as fast as your legs can carry you."

Jones went noiselessly by the side of the fence a distance of a quarter of a mile, and waited for his prey. Between the sharpness of the wind and his rage, his teeth chattered fiercely.

"I shall get him out of the way to-night, and there will be nothing between me and Ann. He shall pay dearly for his boldness. The dirty, low and contemptible wretch, as he is ! What if I am accused of the atrocious deed ? What if my father heard of it ? God only knows—if there is a God. Hush, sentiment ! John Jones, be brave, be a man ! " said he to himself. He then heard unusual rustling in the top of the oak.

"Dear heaven, we are watched," said he, and an owl gave such a loud screech over his head that he nearly fainted.

Presently he heard the sound of feet, and saw a young man walking past and whistling merrily. "There he is," said Jones to himself, and he made haste to join his friends, who were waiting for him.

" He is on his journey," he said. " Be ready, he will be here in ten minutes," and turned to leave them.

" Where is the sack ? " asked one of them wildly.

" Here it is. Everything right then."

CHAPTER VII.

THE POACHERS.—THE TRIAL AND SENTENCE.

"WHERE have you been so long, you lazy rags ? We have been waiting for you for half an hour, and are nearly numb with cold." That was the salutation two young men from Llangynwyd received from their companions when they met in a particular part of the parish. It was evident that they belonged to the poacher fraternity.

" Have you the nets with you ? "

" Yes, and the two dogs."

" All right. As the time is gone far, we may as well begin at once."

" Yes ; sooner the better."

They went a short distance until they came to the brook field, when one of them turned to his friends remarking—

" This is the field. There are three or four of the finest hares I have ever seen. Now, Shanco and Edmont shall go up the top of the field and lay the nets, whilst we go down to the bridge with the two dogs. When the nets are set give the signal, and if you want help whistle in the usual way, and we shall do the same if necessary."

With such instructions the friends separated, the two walking cautiously by the side of the brook to the top of the field. When they reached the bridge, Tom knocked his foot against something, which made him fall. " What is here ? " he asked, feeling with his hands. " Edmont, bring the light at once. Here's a spoil for us."

" What is it ? "

" I cannot tell.   It is something in a sack."

Edmont brought the light, and after examining it carefully asked, in amazement, " What can it be ?   I will
see," and, beginning to open the sack, he exclaimed in a
frightened voice, " Good God !   Some dead man is in the
sack."

" What are you trying to say ? "

" Yes, truly.   Whistle to bring down the others."

Ned obeyed, and in few minutes they were joined by
the others, and the four men stood petrified over what
appeared to be the body of a dead man.

" Who could have placed it here, I wonder ? "

" That's the question."

" Let us have a look at the face to see if we know him,
and decide what to do."

The body was taken out of the sack, and in so doing
they were still more frightened when they heard deep
groans from his breast.

" Great heavens," exclaimed Edmont, " he is my
cousin—Will Hopkin."

" Yes, to be sure.   Let us send for help at once.   He
may not be beyond hope."

Two of them ran to the village, and said that Will
Hopkin had been murdered, and that his body had been
thrown in a sack into the brook.   It is easier to imagine
than describe the effect the terrible news had upon the
inhabitants of the district, and in less than half an hour
there were scores of lights to be seen in the neighbourhood
of the brook.   Will Hopkin was placed on a board, and
carried home by his neighbours.   The doctor, who was
present to meet them, after careful examination pro-

nounced life not extinct, and, applying something from a bottle to his lips, the patient soon began to breathe freely.

Great was the anxiety in the parish to discover who had been guilty of attempting to murder Will, but the efforts were fruitless for weeks. One day a stranger appeared at the village, inquiring for the shop of William Jones. It was pointed out to him, and he went into it. No one happened to be in but John, the son.

" Am I speaking to Mr. Jones, junior ? " asked the stranger.

" Yes, I am John, son of William Jones," whilst at the same time his face turned as white as a whitewashed wall. There was something in the face of the stranger when speaking which made Jones afraid of him.

Said the stranger : " You are the gentleman I wished to see. Perhaps you would go with me into a private room, for I have an important personal matter I wish to speak to you about."

Our old friend scarcely knew what to do, but ran frightened into the house. He was too weak to speak when he reached it, and the only words that were intelligible that fell from his lips were, " Man—shop."

William Jones went into the shop at once, and asked the stranger what he wanted.

" Nothing of importance to you. I want to speak privately to your son, and for that purpose I asked him to go with me for a few minutes to a private room."

" Tell your message to me if you please, sir. It may do as well perhaps as to himself."

" Not altogether. I am bound to speak to your son privately."

There was something in the tone of the stranger which led William Jones to think that to yield to his request was the best, and he was shown into a private room, and the son was sent to him.

" You have come, then ? " said the stranger, as Jones made his appearance.

" Yes, sir," was the reply.

" I will thank you to sit opposite me."

Jones did so.

" Now, is the door locked ? "

" No, but I will bolt it at once."

After doing so, and resuming his seat, the stranger asked him—

" Perhaps you will be kind enough to inform me if you know Ann Thomas, of Cefn Ydfa."

" Yes, very well," Jones replied.

He felt a cold shiver creeping over him as the stranger pronounced, " Cefn Ydfa."

" So.   Do you know Will Hopkin, the thatcher."

" Yes."

" Was Will with her at Bridgend Fair ? "

" Yes."

" Were you there ? "

" Yes."

" Did you see them walking together in the town the day of the fair ? "

" Yes."

" Can you tell if Will Hopkin returned with her that night ? "

" I don't——yes, I think so."

" You saw them returning together then ? "

" No "

" Good God ! some Dead Man is in the sack."

PAGE 40.

" Oh, well.   When did you return from the fair ? "

" I cannot tell what o'clock it was.   It may have been about four in the afternoon."

" It is natural to expect, as a matter of course, that you would be home before seven ? "

" No, it was a little later."

" It may have been nine or ten o'clock ? "

" Yes, a little after ten."

" Did the journey take up all that time ? "

" Yes."

" Do you do much business, Jones ? "

" Oh, yes.   Ours is the largest shop in the place."

" Do you sell much flour ? "

" Yes."

" Of whom do you get your flour ? "

" Williams and Son, Swansea."

" You have it in sacks, of course ? "

" Yes."

" Their own sacks I mean ? "

" Yes."

" Have you any mark by which you can know the sacks of the company ? "

" Yes.   I would know them in a minute."

" Very good," said the stranger, opening a small parcel which he carried under his arm.

Spreading the sack before him on the table, he asked—

" Whose is this ? "

" Williams and Son's," answered Jones, trembling.

It was an excellent opportunity for the pencil of an artist to depict the guilty when caught in his own net. Jones's face had become as pale as that of the king of terrors.   He trembled all over, and a cold perspiration covered his forehead.

The stranger observed these changes in Jones's countenance with an eagle eye.   There was painful silence for some time.   At last the stranger asked—

" Do you know if any of the sacks of the firm have been given out by you lately ? "

" No.   We never allow them to go out of the shop.   We have some of our own to meet the wants of customers, lest Williams's should be lost."

It was evident by this time that Jones did not know what he was saying.   He was quite mixed.

" Well, my friend, I am very sorry for you.   I am afraid that you know something of the recent attack upon William Hopkin, and there is only one course open to me. You must go with me," at the same time taking a pair of handcuffs from his pocket and preparing to put them on.

" Father, father !   Oh, father, come here," shouted Jones.

This brought his father on the scene, who was filled with astonishment upon finding that the stranger had been changed into an officer of the law, and his son Jon handcuffed.

" What does this mean ?   What is the matter ? " he asked wildly.

" I am bound to arrest him on suspicion of being concerned in the attempt to murder William Hopkin. Although many circumstances strengthen the suspicion of his guilt, matters may turn otherwise.   At present I am under the necessity of taking him prisoner ; and you must bear in mind that any opposition on your part would be a breach of the law.   Now, Jones, come along.' And off they went.

Before sunset that day, Bill the ratcatcher and Dai of the Cwm were arrested on suspicion. They were brought before the magistrates, and committed to the assizes on the charge of attempting to murder William Hopkin.

After the committal of the prisoners to the assizes the officers of the law were active in obtaining proofs of their guilt, and they succeeded in securing enough evidence to obtain their conviction. The advocate of the prisoners could not shake the testimony of the witnesses. After the advocate had addressed the jury, the judge summed up :

"There is no doubt," he said, "that the attempt to murder was most barbarous and atrocious, but the question for you, as a jury, is to consider whether the evidence offered is enough to prove that the prisoners at the bar were guilty of it."

The jury retired to consider the evidence, and returned in twenty minutes with a verdict of " Guilty ! " and the prisoners were sentenced to transportation for life. In three weeks the unfortunate men were on board the ship that conveyed them to a distant land, from whence they never returned.

CHAPTER VIII.

WE must now turn our attention towards Cefn Ydfa, to see how matters appear there. As might be expected, the family were much grieved at the brutal attack upon Will Hopkin the night of the fair, but none of them felt so sorry as Ann. Her affection for him was not cooled in the least—if anything, it had increased ; but she endeavoured to conceal her feelings. The time had passed swiftly, the trial was over, and, to her delight, Will was gradually but certainly recovering his strength.

One morning, whilst fetching the cows to be milked her eyes fell on a strange object, near a stile she had to cross. It was coming towards her, and attracted her attention, but she could not tell whether it was a man woman, or some unearthly being. It was covered by a large red cloak, which concealed everything except a little of the face. When it came near, she discovered that it belonged to the female sex, and was one of the wandering gipsies that are often seen in Wales.

Ann was a little frightened when she saw her, which the old woman quickly discovered, and said in a kind voice—

" You need not fear me, my fair lady, for I have done no harm to anybody in my life, and I am not going to begin now. Will you please inform me if I am on the way to the village of Llangynwyd ? "

" You are."

" Thank you.   Who is living in that fine house ? "

" Its owner, my mother, Catherine Thomas."

' Are you her daughter ? "

" You are right."

" The only child, the heiress, I presume ? "

" Yes."

" I pity you, my beautiful girl.   Although light of
heart to-day, there are years of affliction and trouble in
store for you, because of your love and attachment to a
young labouring man."

Ann laughed heartily when she heard the announce-
ment, and thought the old woman was mad.

" Our fate in the future is so shrouded in impenetrable
darkness that we canot tell what may happen, and you
do not appear to know more of the future than I do."

The old woman pointed her hand towards Ann, saying
—" A young woman sinking to the grave of the broken-
hearted in the spring of her life because compelled to
marry a man she does not love."   With the last word she
disappeared in the wood, but her form remained before
Ann's eyes, and the sound of her terrible words haunted
her for a long time.

" But what did the old gipsy know ?   She was probably
mad."

That was what filled the mind of the Maid of Cefn Ydfa
throughout the day.

A young gentleman, son of a wealthy lawyer, paid a
visit to Cefn Ydfa that afternoon.   He had been known
to the family for years, but had never called at the house
before.   He was a well-built young man, of gentlemanly
appearance, and about twenty-one, dressed in the latest
fashion, and his manner and speech indicated that he

considered himself above the common. He had, in addition, received the best education that could be obtained in that age, and was fond of giving practical illustrations of his knowledge. How extensive was his learning we do not know ; but his babbling about it was enough to sicken any man. " Empty vessels make the most noise," says the old Welsh proverb, and we might infer the same of persons who boast of their profound (?) knowledge, whilst at the same time they are as ignorant as a mole. It appears that this fellow had spent some time at an English school, and whatever progress he had made in various branches of learning, he had learned to perfection to speak Welsh with the affectation of Dick-Shon-Dafydd, and depreciate Welsh scenery and the habits of the people, and the superiority of the children of Hengist over his own countrymen. These characteristics did not induce the honest family of Cefn Ydfa to form a high opinion of him—indeed, Ann disliked him from the first time she saw him. It was evident that his chief object in all his babblings was to attract attention towards himself and what he said. She watched his movements very carefully and could not conceal her contempt for him now and then.

Some time in the afternoon, her mother requested her to go and milk the cows, because the servant girl had gone from home.

" Which cows do you mean ? " asked Ann.

" Why, those in the upper cowhouse, girl. How stupid you are," said the mother.

" Very well, mother, I will go at once."

" Would it be too great a favour to ask to be allowed to accompany you, Miss Thomas ? " asked the visitor.

" Not in the least, Mr. Maddock. You are welcome."

Ann had already guessed the object of his visit, and now she was confirmed in the impression, and was prepared to meet his advances. They were soon on the narrow path leading to the cowhouse, when he said :

" What a rough and stony path ? "

" Yes, but I do not find it so. But that is to be attributed perhaps to my constant use of it," she replied drily.

" It is enough to make the feet of a giant sore."

" I do not think so, for I suffer no inconvenience whilst walking over it. But why should I talk ? I am only a country girl, brought up in one of the Welsh mountains and have no experience, consequently, of the thin and light shoes of the English," said Ann with scorn.

" The habits of the English much excel, in everything, the awkward ways of the Welsh."

" If so, it is a wonder that you should have left such a perfect nation."

" H'm ! There is a reason for everything, or, probably I should not have left."

The conversation ceased. It was evident that there was something important resting on the young man's mind.

After Ann had finished milking, and whilst preparing to return to the house, the young man gently took the maiden's hand, and said :

" Excuse me, most beautiful of Eve's daughters, I have long wished to have the opportunity of unburdening my heart, which has been possessed ever since the first time my eyes saw your angelic face. Miss Thomas, I cannot conceal my feelings a moment longer. I love you with my whole heart."

" I am afraid that you have concealed your love for me too long. My word is passed to him who has won my heart, and to whom I shall be faithful whilst I live."

" Who is that fortunate individual ? "

" That is my business. I do not consider it my duty to name him now."

" Is it Will Hopkin, the thatcher ? "

" Mr. Maddock, I have always looked upon you as a young man blessed with advantages out of the common ; let not your conduct lead me to think less of you. Let the matter rest where it is."

" But consider, Miss Thomas, that you are a rich heiress, whilst—

" Sir, say no more on the subject. I have given you my answer, and there is no power in existence that would compel me to withdraw a word I have said, and I shall therefore thank you to leave me alone."

" Oh, cruel Miss Thomas ! How can you be so un- feeling towards one who loves you so dearly ? "

" My conduct is not cruel or unfeeling. It would be so if I gave my word to you, and say that I love you and do not. Let the matter rest where it is."

" Am I to consider your answer final and unchange- able ? " said the young man.

" Yes, if you wish to retain my friendship, say no more about it," was her dry answer.

The young man bent his head, and said nothing.

Shortly afterwards they returned to the house, and whilst crossing the field they saw a lame youth, leaning upon a stick, coming towards them ; and when he came near, they recognised him. Whilst Ann welcomed him as the idol of her heart, the young man who accompanied her regarded him as his greatest enemy. He was Will Hopkin, the poet. Maddock passed him as if he had not seen him, but Ann remained to speak to him.

It was a heavy blow for the profound scholar to receive such a firm and uncompromising answer from Ann ; and to meet his opponent, when his heart was bleeding from the sting of her words, added greatly to the pain that possessed him. He walked briskly across the field, and, on looking backward whilst crossing the stile, he saw Will embracing Ann, and printing a number of kisses upon her rosy cheeks.

"Are matters to be allowed to take this course without a protest ? " he asked himself.

With disappointment spread over his face, like a veil, he entered the house.

CHAPTER IX.

THE CONSEQUENCE.

THE Maid of Cefn Ydfa was fatherless. She had no recollection of him, for he had died when she was an infant about three years of age. One of his principal friends was William Maddock, who lived at a place called Cwmyrisgla, about three miles from Cefn Ydfa. He was a retired lawyer by profession, who had inherited considerable property from his uncle. William Thomas, of Cefn Ydfa, died suddenly. When returning from Bridgend market he felt great pain in his head, and by great efforts he reached home and went at once to bed, from which he never rose. A doctor was sent for at once ; but, notwithstanding every attention, the patient sank rapidly. When the doctor saw there was no hope, he recommended his patient to make his will, in order to save trouble thereafter. He consented, and the will was made and sealed, in which he left all he possessed to his only child Ann, and, appointing her mother and his friend William Maddock, trustees over her until she reached twenty-one, and gave them power to do the best they could for her. And to the honour of William Maddock it is proper to state that a more honest and faithful trustee never lived. His experience enabled him to form a fair value of the estates of Cefn Ydfa. Maddock had a son, who was a few years older than the heiress of Cefn Ydfa ; and he thought, no doubt, that the union of his son Anthony with the wealthy heiress a desirable consummation. This fact, no doubt, influenced him to be so honest and careful in the discharge of his duties as trustee. One afternoon, whilst on a visit to Cefn Ydfa, he mentioned to Mrs. Thomas that his son Anthony had just returned from school for the holidays. She said that she would like to see him, and invited him to call before he returned. He felt very much pleased with the invitation. He saw that his son would come into closer intimacy with the heiress, and, perhaps, win her affections, and thus unite the two families. The reader will remember, from reading the former chapter, that the young man's proposal was rejected. His non-success had a serious effect upon him, and he appeared very depressed when he returned home. His father thought his son was suffering from some indisposition, and questioned him about it ; but he answered, with a degree of unconcern, that there was nothing the matter with him. After more careful observation, the father suspected the cause, and asked his son if he had seen Ann.

" Yes," he answered, lowering his head. " I think it would have been better for me if I had not spoken to her."

" Now I understand why you have looked so gloomily the last few days, my son. She refused you. Take courage, I will look into the matter."

A smile passed over the son's countenance when his father had spoken.

" I will write," added Mr. Maddock, " to Mrs. Thomas, informing her of the circumstance, and if her daughter does not act more prudently in future, I have the power in my hands to disinherit her of the estate of Cefn Ydfa. I was appointed by her father to watch her, and use my authority as I thought best. All the papers and documents relating to the estate are in my possession ; but neither she nor her mother know it. I will send John, the servant, with the letter this afternoon. Make your mind easy ; matters will soon be right."

The son retired from the room smiling pleasantly.

A little before sunset that afternoon, a person appeared before the door of Cefn Ydfa holding a large sealed letter in his hand, and asking for Mrs. Thomas. One of the servants answered that she was in, and went to inform her mistress of the presence of the stranger. Mrs. Thomas came from the kitchen, and the messenger handed her the letter, and left. She went into the parlour, broke the seal, and read its contents, which were as follows :—

" Madam,—I write to you to-day in a different spirit to when I last wrote to you. As you are aware, I was appointed by the late Mr. Thomas a trustee over your daughter Ann, until she is twenty-one. And, by careful attention to my obligations, I have succeeded in discharging the heavy debts that rested on the Cefn Ydfa Estate ; and I have placed £5,000 in her name at the Bank at Bridgend—to be paid her, with interest, when she comes of age. I have watched her affairs with such care as if she had been my own child. But the manner in which both of you treated my son, when on a visit to your house, shows that you do not value my services, or even thank me for them. I now beg to inform you that none of the papers and documents, which place your daughter in possession of the estate, are in your possession, and no one but myself knows where they are hidden and it rests entirely with me whether she will inherit the estate of her ancestors or not. I warn you both to be wiser in your conduct in the future, lest ingratitude should bring forth serious consequences.—I am, WILLIAM MADDOCK. Cwmyrisgla, Thursday."

Had a thunderbolt fallen in the room by her side, Mrs. Thomas would not have been more frightened than by the contents of this letter. She did not know what to do, and called her daughter and showed her the letter. The daughter appeared as if paralysed by its wonderful and unexpected contents. After a little consideration she related to her mother what had passed between her and Anthony Maddock when returning from milking the cows.

" I see," said her mother, " the cause of the letter, but cannot help being surprised that a person in Mr. Maddock's position should threaten revenge because you refused his son as a sweetheart. We must put our heads together, and act seriously at once. What about the title deeds of the estate and the will of your father ? I do not remember ever having seen them."

" Nor I," said Ann. " I did not know that they were in existence."

" They must be somewhere, but the question is where is that ' somewhere ? ' "

" They may be among the papers and writings on skins in the large box in the upper loft."

" Perhaps. We will search for them to-morrow."

It was so agreed. As it may be expected, the remainder of that day was very anxious and unhappy for the mother and daughter. But Ann was consoled by the fact that there was one who loved her, and whom she loved in return.

That night a young man might have been seen crossing the small lawn in front of the house, walking cautiously towards one of the windows, which he lightly tapped. Immediately, a beautiful young girl emerged from the house, and went to the spot where stood the young man, who, as soon as her saw her, opened wide his arms, into which she threw herself at once. There was a good deal of hugging and kissing without a word spoken. There is a language without words. It can be read in the cheerful eye of the maiden, through her tears, like the sunbeams after a shower in May—the earth smiled on the sun and the sun smiled through the rain clouds upon the earth. So were the heiress of Cefn Ydfa and Will Hopkin the Bard. Pure love and affection filled their hearts, which was evident by the ardent manner they embraced, and when his lips pressed her rosy cheeks, with trembling lips she told him of the threats of William Maddock because she refused to accept his son as a lover.

" Never mind, Ann. If the knave succeeds in disinheriting you of the property of your ancestors, I shall be true to you whatever may be the consequences. These arms shall defend you while any strength remains in them, and no bitter breeze shall blow upon you without first passing over me. My affection for you would remain as ardent if you were not worth one halfpenny," said the young man.

" Then I am not mistaken. You really love me, Will ?" she whispered.

" A thousand times more than my life," said he, drawing her towards him, and pressing his lips to hers. They soon separated after a renewed pledge of their fidelity to each other.

Next morning, as arranged, Mrs. Thomas and her daughter commenced a search of the old family papers, and the dust from them was enough to stifle anyone. Notwithstanding a long search, they did not come across what they wanted. Dinner time arrived, and they gave it up for a time. After dinner they resumed their work, and were engaged until the evening, and then abandoned it in despair.

"They are nowhere in the house," observed Mrs. Thomas, "and they must be with Mr. Maddock."

"How did he dare take them from here?" asked Ann.

"He took advantage of it when I was in such trouble after the death of your father. My mind was in such a state that I paid no attention to anything. The day of the funeral—oh, such a day! I shall not forget that memorable day as long as I live! The recollection of its incidents are quite fresh in my memory!"

She covered her face with her hands and cried. There was a painful suspense for a time. The first to break the silence was Ann, who asked if they could do anything more.

"I must go over to Cwmyrisgla to see Mr. Maddock," was the reply, "and to get the documents from him if possible."

"What shall we do if he should refuse?"

"Oh, I scarcely think he would be so unjust as to refuse so reasonable a request. But he is an old lawyer, and may keep them until you are twenty-one, when he would be bound to give them up."

It was so arranged.

Mrs. Thomas went next day on her important mission, and as Mr. Maddock's residence was not far off it took her but a short time to reach it. She remained there all day.

It was an anxious day for Ann. Mrs. Thomas returned about five o'clock, and it was evident from the pleased smile on her countenance that she was satisfied, and this added to Ann's anxiety. Just as she entered the house, a message came from the family of Ty-isaf, that Billy, an old labourer on the estate, was taken ill that afternoon and likely to die. He begged to see his mistress, and without taking off her bonnet she went at once to visit the sick man. Billy was a widower having buried his wife, and never was a more faithful servant at Cefn Ydfa, or anywhere else. Taking charge of the house and of the children was an old maid, noted for her faithfulness even among the women of that age. When Mrs. Thomas reached the house, she went at once to the sick chamber, but Billy was unable to recognise her. His senses were gone. When leaving the room, Mrs. Thomas asked the old housekeeper what was the matter with her master.

" He may pull through it," was the answer." I am afraid that he has hard times before him."

" He is only comparatively young, and has a strong constitution, and may recover."

" Perhaps so," said the old servant with emphasis, " but I am afraid of it. We have something here last night which I don't like, to say the least of it."

" What was it ? " asked Mrs. Thomas anxiously.

The old girl approached near her, and said in low tones, " You know our old sheepdog ? "

" Quite well."

" Well, last night it was impossible to get it into the house, and after much coaxing we gave it up, and we left it in the garden, and there it howled piteously all night. It was impossible to sleep on account of the mournful howling. When I rose this morning I looked through the window, and the first thing I saw was a large hole dug under the apple tree in the garden in front of the house. As soon as I dressed I went out, and it corresponded, to my surprise, to the size and form of a grave."

" Do you think that the dog dug it ? " asked Mrs. Thomas, in astonishment.

" I am certain of it."

" What could have moved it to do it ? "

" It is a sign of an early death in the family. Dogs are blessed with more true knowledge of the future than we are."

" It is surprising that an irrational creature should be possessed of more knowledge than rational beings."

" It is so, but it is quite true. I have taken notice of them often, and could relate many instances of strange things that have happened in my time, and of which I have been an eye-witness. But death is not certain to take place at once, and some months may elapse, but it is certain to occur within the year."

" And you think that the action of the dog last night forebodes the death of your master ? "

" I am not certain of it, but I don't like it."

Mrs. Thomas left the superstitious old woman, and went home. When she reached the house, she went into the parlour and sent for her daughter. They were closeted a long time, and the conversation between them was of a private nature ; but when Ann came out, her eyes were red with crying, and she appeared depressed and heartless. What was the cause ? The two servant maids noticed the sudden change in her countenance, and came to the conclusion that it was due to the interview

in the parlour. Poor Ann ! that was the first of a long
series of troubles which ceased not until she had passed
from this troublesome world. She soon retired to her
room, and threw herself upon her bed, where the flood-
gates of her hidden·grief burst, and in the solitude of the
night she might be heard crying—

"Oh ! merciful heaven, is it to be so ? Is there no
deliverance ? My God, have mercy upon me ! "

What was the cause of her grief ?

CHAPTER X.

THE PRESS GANG.—ATTEMPT TO INDUCE WILL HOPKIN
TO ENLIST.

THE inhabitants of the seashores of Glamorganshire
were visited in olden times by the officers of the
pressgang. They were feared by every class and age.
It was only necessary to mention the pressgang to
frighten everybody. The pressgang was the bugbear of
the neighbourhood in which I was born. I remember
that the very mention of it brought me to obey at once.

One day, whilst Will Hopkin was busy at his work of
thatching in the village of Llangynwyd, he was addressed
by name. He turned his head, and saw, to his great surprise, a tall young man standing on the roadway before
him. Will asked what he wanted of him.

"Nothing particularly, only I want to have a talk with
you."

Will came down from the ladder, and the stranger
asked him a large number of questions about the place
and its inhabitants. After exhausting his store of questions in that direction, he began to ask about himself
and his personal affairs, adding that it was a pity that a
young man so smart as he was should be obliged to follow
the humble occupation of thatcher. Will said that he
was satisfied with his condition, and could not understand
what it mattered to other people. The stranger laughed,
or attempted to laugh, saying—"I should think that you
value your calling very much."

" Yes, better than any other," was the answer.

" But if you had the offer of more profitable and honourable employment would you not accept it ? "

" That would depend entirely upon its nature. If I considered it more profitable and more honourable, it is more than likely that I would accept it ; at any rate, I would not stand in my own light."

" Have you ever felt a wish to go to sea ? "

" No ; and it is not likely that I shall. I would a thousand times rather remain on land, although the employment were poor, than risk my life on the furrowed back of ' Davy Jones.' "

The young man shook hands with Will, and put a shilling quietly in his hand. Will could not guess what it meant, but his imagination was soon at work to find it out, and suspicions rose in his breast. Whilst thinking over the matter, he heard someone calling loudly upon him, and, upon his turning round, saw Jack the Carrier riding leisurely on the back of his donkey, with a short pipe in his mouth, whilst in his hand he held a stick, not unlike the Irishman's shillalagh, which, it was understood, was the constant visitor of the western part of his long-eared companion. He stood by the house on which Will was working, asking how he was.

" Oh, pretty well," answered Will, preparing to descend.

" How are matters towards Cefn Ydfa just now ? I hear that you often visit the place."

" Everything is just as it was, and every member of the family takes its daily food, as far as I know."

" How is Ann ? "

" Like what she used to be---if any, she improves daily in loveliness."

" I have heard there is a new candidate for her hand, who has recently made his appearance."

" Not a word."

" Well, there is one, and, to say the least, who will prove himself a bitter and dangerous opponent. His position, and the influence of his father upon the family of Cefn Ydfa, are to be feared."

" Who can he be ? "

" Anthony Maddock, of Cwmyrisgla ; and I am informed from a source upon which I can rely that Mrs. Thomas favours him."

" I cannot believe it. It is an unfounded rumour."

" Well, I am afraid there is much truth in it ; and you may depend upon it that he will prove a bitter enemy to you. And, as his father is one of the trustees appointed by her father over Ann, you may depend he will use his power and authority to force her to marry his son."

" I did not know that William Maddock was one of the trustees before."

" Yes, he is."

" Who told you ? "

" Mary, the servant. Mrs. Thomas was at Cwmyrisgla on Monday, and when she returned she commanded Ann to join her in the parlour ; and they remained together for two hours. When Ann returned to the kitchen her eyes showed that she had been crying about something, and the cheerfulness which usually characterised her is gone, and she was evidently in great trouble. The servants could not tell what was the matter, but they thought that the visit to the Cwm had something to do with it."

" What could it be, I wonder ? "

" I have mentioned it already, and it is the common talk of the neighbourhood that Anthony Maddock is courting Ann, of Cefn Ydfa. But I cannot say what truth there is in it ; everything is in the mist just now." And, with the application of the shillalagh to the back of Andro, Jack went away, leaving Will in confusion.

It is unnecessary for me to state, for the reader can imagine, what filled the mind of the young thatcher during the remainder of the day.

" Is Ann faithful ?   No, she has deceived me !   She is a deceitful girl !   No, how can I call her deceitful, whilst my conscience says that I have no right to question the vows she has voluntarily made to me, or a right to darken the life of a youthful maiden by bringing her down to a poor and humble station like mine." This is how Will thought.   He resolved to see her that night, and in the light of the cold moon he wended his way towards her residence.   He was not long before he had the chief object of his affections in his arms.   He related to her the circumstances of the day, and what he had heard, as well as his anxiety in relation to them.

" Ann," said he, " I beg you not to conceal the truth from me.   Don't deceive me."

" Will ! this from you, of all people ! Have you ever had reason to suspect that I am not true to you ? "

" Never, my darling."

" No, and you never will.   There are grounds for what you have heard.   William Maddock is doing all in his power to induce me to accept his son as my lover, and has gone so far as to suggest that I should look upon him as my future husband.   But I have turned a deaf ear to him.   I will not be tempted by his fair words, or frightened by his threats ; and you may depend, dear Will, that I will prove true to my vows that I swear to you, whatever the consequences may be."

The young bard said nothing, but drew her closer to his bosom, and looked through his tears upon her beautiful face.

" Will," she said again, " whatever you may hear about me take no notice of it. Trust me. We will remain the same to the end. My mind will never change. Fine weather follows rain, and the cloud that now hangs threateningly over our heads will be scattered."

They soon separated, and Will went home with a troubled mind.

Next day, whilst busy at his work, the stranger whom he met the previous day made his appearance, accompanied by another official. They approached him, and began a conversation about indifferent matters. Will was very abrupt in his answers. One of them remark that it was a pity that he should follow such a calling, and that it would be better for him to accompany them to the sea ; whereupon Will said that he had told his mind upon the matter the day before, and that he had not changed his opinion. They went away, and Will learnt that they were the officers of the pressgang stationed at Swansea.

That afternoon, after returning home, Will's mother handed him a letter which had been brought by a lad. He recognised the handwriting as that of the fair maid of Cefn Ydfa. With a trembling hand he broke the seal and looked at its contents. An observant person might have seen from his countenance that it contained matters of importance. It read thus :—

" My dear Will,—With a trembling hand I write this note. Be on your guard, for the enemy is at work already. It is not, necessary for me to name him. He believes that you are the cause why I refused his son, and he thinks that if he can get you out of the way he would succeed in his object. But he is greatly mistaken, and shall know it. They have some scheme on hand against you, but I don't know what it is. I only heard a word this morning ; and, worse than all, they have persuaded my mother, by some trickery, to favour it. But it makes no difference—their schemes will not reach the object they have in view. Don't forget to come here to-morrow night. I am bound to see you, for my peace and honour and your future are all in the scale now. I shall wait for you in the greenhouse at eight o'clock.—This from your faithful ANN."

What has caused such an earnest appeal ? Is there another bitter storm brewing ? He determined to observe her request, and hear the truth from her own lips.

CHAPTER XI.

"IT is no use to attempt to persuade him to join us by air means. We must, if you wish to get rid of him, adopt more effective means."

"I do not understand you. Speak more plainly."

"We are speaking plainly enough to enable anyone possessed of ordinary understanding to realise what we mean. We must devise some means to get him into a snare, and then pounce upon him unexpectedly, and take him secretly away. There is no mistake about it."

The foregoing conversation took place in a small coppice on Cwmyrisgla land on a fine afternoon in May. The company consisted of three men. Two of them might be recognised by their seafaring garments, while the third was a young man of a proud and conceited bearing.

"I am afraid that that would be too dangerous a plan to attempt."

"Not in the least. We could bring it about without any living man knowing it ; and we assure you, if you place the matter in our hands, and come up to the terms, we shall not leave it unfinished. He will be too far from you in a fortnight to cause you any trouble."

"Of course, to get him out of the way so that I may secure my purpose is my wish ; and he may return afterwards as soon as he likes, as far as I am concerned."

" Do you agree to the terms or not ?   Decide at once, one way or another."

" How much do you want ? "

" Two hundred guineas."

" Are you serious ? "

" As serious as if we were going to be hung."

" The amount is much too large.   Say one hundred."

" Not a farthing under two hundred, sir.   You need not attempt to reduce it, for it would simply be a waste of time."

" It would be better for you to take the hundred.   Consider to whom you are talking, and behave more respectfully ;   you may have cause to repent of your crime, should it be made public."

" Ha ! ha !   We have heard persons speaking boastingly before.   But we know how to bring them to their senses, and teach them to keep a secret for ever.   Do you see this," said one of them, taking a pistol from his pocket, and pointing it towards the young man—" Here is a schoolmaster that will teach you how to keep a secret ; and, since we have had such a manifestation of your character, we beg to inform you that, unless we get three hundred guineas, you will not see the sun now setting rising again.   Do you understand, sir ? "

It was evident that the young man was so frightened that he could not speak.   His face was pale, and head bent, without an idea what to do.   He saw that he was in the hands of cut-throats.

" You intend to kill me ? " he asked.

" Nothing of the kind if you agree to the terms we have laid down.   If you don't, and having brought us to such a pass, there is nothing left but to give you a lesson on the importance of holding your tongue. The lesson is costly, it is true, for it means your life. But if you are prepared to be advised by us, you had better yield, and kiss the rod."

" Will you allow me until to-morrow evening to consider the matter ? "

" Not a moment. You have, as we have said already, disclosed your character too plainly for us to let you go. Do you accept our terms, or not ? "

" It appears as if I had better accept them, bad as they are. But I have not the two hundred pounds with me."

" Three hundred, if you please, sir."

" Two hundred was the first condition ! "

'True, but we found out that we were dealing with a knave, and we thought it fair to deal a little knavish with him, and, as knaves, we stick to the terms. It matters not whether you have the money by you or not. Your name at the bottom of this paper will do quite as well," said one of them, taking out a paper from his pocket.

" But I should like to know what are the contents of the paper before I put my name to it. It may be for a thousand guineas as far as I know."

" Not a farthing more than three hundred guineas. You may rely upon our word. Although you are not allowed to see everything that is written on the paper since you are so suspicious, you shall see part of it," he said, half-opening the paper.

The young man made no further objections, and signed his name at the bottom.

" Now that that is over, you will perhaps inform me how you propose to proceed ? "

" That is our business. Leave that to us. Enough for you to be certain he is got out of the way."

" Yes, yés, I shall be quite satisfied."

" Now we must move," and the two men disappeared in the forest, leaving the young gentleman alone.

Shortly afterwards, the smallest of the two asked the other,—" What do you think of him ? "

" Only that he is very silly," was the reply.

" Yes, is he not ? "

" Do you think that he has any idea who I am ? "

" Not in the least, not more than the man with the load of thorns in the moon."

" H'm ! I am glad to hear that. Three hundred guineas ! A large sum for a small job."

" Yes."

" I wonder if his father is on the land of the living now ? "

" I have heard that he is, and that he lives with his father."

" So. I should like to meet old Maddock somewhere privately. I would soon make his power of speech useless to him. That bit of land of my mother—the Gelly—rests heavily on my mind. The unprincipled thief that he is ! I may have the opportunity of repaying him again. But perhaps it is better not to think of the past. I have but little comfort from the recollection of my early life."

He spoke the last sentences more to himself than to his companion ; and it was evident that the scenes which surrounded him awoke remembrances of the past, and many a sigh escaped from his breast. Shortly afterwards, the youngest of the two remarked that they had better remain in the forest until their friends joined them.

" Yes. Here is a safe place. What time is it ? "

" It is half-past seven."

" So we have an hour and a half to wait ? "

" Yes."

" Are you sure they will come to meet us ? "

" Unless some unexpected difficulty intervenes."

" No. Anthony has promised to lodge him safely for the night, and he will remain there till to-morrow night, when he will be put on board ship."

" When do you propose to lift the sails ? "

" The first tide the day after to-morrow."

They were some time afterwards silent. The night was closing, and the birds sang their evening carol from the trees, and, now and then, the voice of the cuckoo was heard. Nature appeared like a young maiden, light-footed and mirthful, and the trees were arraying themselves in their tender green foliage. Although everything in nature appeared cheerful, the elder of the two men was not at ease. The cloud that sat over him showed that he was not happy. He turned about uneasily.

" The time is nearly up," said the younger.

" Well, we had better start ; " and off they went. After reaching a small bush, not far from Cefn Ydfa, they were met by two men, one of whom was the young man who had arranged the terms shortly before, whilst the other was an old man. The eldest of the officers looked at him carefully, as if to bring to his recollection where he had seen him before ; but he was not long before his countenance changed, and his eyes flashed with anger, and it was with an effort that he held his tongue from giving expression to what convulsed his heart.

" You have come," said one of them.

" Yes."

" Very good.   He will be here in half an hour.   We hope you are prepared."

" Yes, we are quite ready."

They separated, and each one took his place waiting the person they expected.

CHAPTER XII.

THE PRISONER.—THE DELIVERANCE.

THE appointed time had arrived when the Maid of Cefn Ydfa went silently, like a shadow, to the small greenhouse, where she had requested her lover to meet her. She was closely enveloped in a black cloak, showing only her pale face, the silver beams of the moon making her countenance appear unearthly.

" You have come," said Will Hopkin, who was waiting for her, as she entered.

She took no notice of him, and went to the furthest part of the greenhouse, and took her seat not far from where he sat.

" I imagine you must have something special and important to communicate by your asking for such an unexpected meeting," said Will, after she sat down.

" You are right," she said. " Only——"

But before she had time to finish the sentence the sound of persons quickly walking towards them were heard. In a moment they were at the door, when he who appeared the leader said to his companions—

" He is sure to be here. Let me go in and bring him out," and began to enter.

Will Hopkin was on his feet ready to give him a warm reception, and as the intruder put his head in, Will's fist met it with such force that he fell like a log. When the others saw what had befallen their companion they rushed at Will, and, succeeding in making a prisoner of him, were soon on their journey.

*　　*　　*　　*　　*　　*　　*　　*

It was midnight, and Will sat in a dark and miserable cell. Overcome with astonishment, strange thoughts passed through his brain. Where was Ann ? Was she safe ? Why was he confined in that cell ? He at times suspected Ann of having betrayed him. " But I cannot believe it ; it cannot be," he would say to himself. He rose from the bench upon which he sat, and groped about in search of the door. It was locked, and there was no hope of release, and, sitting down, bitter tears forced themselves to his eyes as the incidents of the night seemed to cast shadows upon his future, and he could not see a single hopeful star. It was not surprising that the spirit of the youthful thatcher should give way.

Whilst thus musing he heard sounds underneath, and listening attentively for a minute or two, he came to the conclusion that it was mice ; but again the sound came nearer to him, and he heard the bolt of his cell withdrawn. He was so frightened that he could not move hand or foot.

" Will ! Will ! " said a trembling but familiar voice, to him, outside the door. " Don't be afraid, I am here— Ann." Next moment the door was opened, and the Maid of Cefn Ydfa entered, and sank, fatigued, on the bench, whilst Will was struck with such wonder that he did not recognise at first the face of his lovely Ann.

" Will, don't you know me ? " whispered Ann.

" My dear Ann," said Will, in a mournful tone, " What has brought you here this time of the night ? How could you risk such danger for one so unworthy ? Leave me

The Young Bard was struck with wonder.

at once in my miserable condition. Your presence only adds to my pain."

She had fully overcome her fright by this time, and felt safe in the company of the one she loved above all others. His hopeless appearance roused her deepest sympathy.

" I fear you do not love me, Will," said she, placing her hand upon his shoulder, her eyes full of tears. " I will not leave you until you are out of danger, and shall never forget you, Will. The remembrance of the delightful hours we have spent together will be the source of my comfort until we meet again. Will it not add to your pleasure ? "

" Dear Ann," cried Will, whilst the tears dimmed his eyes upon observing her fidelity, " whilst I live—until the beatings of my heart cease in death—you, and you only, will be the object of my affections. Your image will never be absent from my sight for ever. But I shall never act unworthily of your love. I shall do nothing that will bring shame to your countenance because you have given your hand to a poor thatcher, unworthy of the affections of so virtuous an angel. I must submit to my fate, and meet the dangers that surround me with the resolution which can only be possessed by one whose heart is pure."

" But my time is very short, Will. You must escape, and do it at once. It is my mission here."

He shook his head. " Impossible, Ann. And if I failed in the attempt I could not live afterwards."

" But you are bound to try. You cannot but succeed," she said excitedly. " And besides, listen to me, I will bear all the responsibility. There is a secret passage from this room to the stable. My mare, Bess, is there waiting for you ready saddled, and don't spare her until you are far enough from your enemies, and then let her find her way home ; but if she does not there is no difference, she will have done a service more than her value by rescuing one who is a thousand times more valuable in the estimation of her mistress than anything on the face of the green earth," she added, smiling sadly. " But you must hasten, for it is not far from the break of dawn. Are you ready ? ".

" Ann, I love you ; my affection for you is undying. I am entirely in your hands ; I will do what you command," said Will.

" I know—I know that well enough," she answered modestly, " and heaven is witness that I appreciate your love and steadfastness at their true value, and you may rest assured that I shall not change in your absence. I know there are trials and temptations before me, but I shall not act unworthy of you—my heart will never change ! But our time is short, and there is not a moment to lose. We have spent too much time already. Be quick, Will ; and remember, after we leave this place, you must follow me in silence. Don't whisper a word, or we are done for. I have arranged to remove everything in the way of our escape. Trust me, and condescend to do the smallest thing I suggest."

Will stood looking with admiration upon her for a time, and then embraced her, and there was much endearing and kissing in that cold and humble cell. They forgot their trouble in the excitement of the moment of pure and genuine love. There is no place too dark or too lonely for mutual affection to manifest itself.

" Heaven bless my Ann, the loveliest and sweetest of womankind," said Will, on separating from her.

" And may every blessing crown thee, Will."

She then proceeded with the small lamp in her hand, followed by Will.

"We must leave everything as we found it," whispered Ann, whilst searching for a small spring in the door. "Here it is," she said, pressing it, and the door closed without any noise. The journey was not long, but it was a serious and anxious time for both of them whilst approaching the stable, and the heart throbs of the maiden were audible on her pointing the lamp in that direction. The splendid animal was ready, and in instinctive sympathy with her mistress and the fugitive she did not welcome them with the usual neighing.

CHAPTER XIII.

THE ATMOSPHERE DARKENING.

NEXT morning, on the servant of Cefn Ydfa entering the private cell, it was found that Will Hopkin. the prisoner, had disappeared without leaving any trace behind him. The servant returned at once to inform Maddock and Mrs. Thomas of what had happened. It is easier to imagine than describe the effect the unexpected news had upon Maddock. He appeared so charged with rage that he could not express himself intelligibly.

" The devil has been helping him, or he never could have escaped," he said.

He had scarcely finished the sentence, when a messenger arrived stating that Bess, Ann's mare, with Maddock's saddle and bridle upon her, had been taken away during the night, and at this his anger reached its extremity. He foamed at the mouth and uttered fierce threats, interspersed with frightful oaths.

" The contemptible devil that he is ! But he shall pay dearly for his daring," said he. He ordered the horses to be saddled in order to follow him, but Mrs. Thomas persuaded him not to do so by hinting that he would not give them any more trouble, and that it would be better to leave him alone.

" But who assisted him ? There must have been some one or more acquainted with the place, for he never could get out himself. How did he come to know the private spring in the door of the cell, which I placed there with my own hands ? "

There was no reply to the question, for there was no one present who knew. It was evident that none of the servants had anything to do with it, and consequently that either Ann or himself had found it out. It was thought that the latter was the most likely, although Maddock had a strong suspicion of Ann.

" Well, let the devil take his chance, and I hope that my eyes will never rest upon him again," said Maddock, " although it would be gratifying to see him placed in the hands of the officers of the law that he might be punished; yet, it is better perhaps that things have turned out as they have, and we will say nothing about it lest the news become general."

" Yes, better leave everything as it is," said Mrs. Thomas.

Ann was not present when this conversation took place between her mother and Maddock. A little before dinner, she was called into the parlour to see her mother. She went at once, guessing the object.

" You wish to see me, mother ? " she asked.

" Yes. I have important news to tell you. Mr. Anthony Maddock has informed me of his desire to marry you, and has asked my consent, and after serious consideration of the matter I have consented, and nothing will give me greater pleasure than to see you both united in holy matrimony. You are about the same age, and he is heir to a considerable estate, as you are, and you have known each other since you were children. Now, Ann, I want you to accept him as your future husband."

" Never ! " answered Ann, without hesitation. " I am truly sorry to cross you in anything, mother, especially in a matter so important as that. But I cannot promise to marry Anthony Maddock."

"Ann, do you, my daughter, my heiress, think to do as you like in a matter so important ? It is utterly unreasonable and below every consideration. The matter is settled, and my answer has been given, and will not be altered by the whim of a wild and thoughtless girl."

"And my answer has been given also, and that will not be changed," Ann said, with self-possession.

"It shall. It must be changed," said the mother, angrily raising her voice.

"My mother, I beg of you not to quarrel. My refusal to marry Anthony Maddock is a matter I have seriously thought of before. We have lived together nearly twenty years without a cross word between us, and I implore you, my dear mother, not to let this matter become a cause of unpleasantness between us, for there is no power in the universe that could induce me to marry a man whom I despise and hate from the bottom of my heart."

"Hate him—despise him !" cried the mother, as if she were too much paralysed to find words to express her mind, on seeing the resoluteness of her daughter.

"Ann," said she, after awhile, "I cannot find words to express my displeasure and astonishment at your disgraceful conduct, and yet I am prepared to pass the matter over and to excuse you for using such disrespectful words about a gentleman whom I consider possessed of sufficient worth to be your husband, and your rebellion against my will."

"But, dear mother, how am I to account for the change that has come over you of late ? Why should you be in favour of a person now whom you formerly ridiculed ? What is the reason ? "

" It is not answering questions about the past is our business now ; leave the past alone, and let us act more wisely in the future. I have settled the question and given my word to Anthony Maddock, and it will never be altered."

" Neither will my resolution ever be changed, you may depend upon it. I would rather a thousand times die an old maid, or get my living as a servant girl, than consent to a union so unnatural and sinful, and swearing false vows. I do not, and cannot bring myself to love Anthony Maddock as a wife should love her husband."

" And am I to take this as your final and unchangeable answer in the matter, Ann ? You are determined to oppose my wishes to the utmost, and thereby refuse an offer that would honour even the heiress of Cefn Ydfa."

" Excuse me for differing from you about the matter. I do not consider the ' offer,' as you call it, anything less than an insult, and it will certainly be so regarded if it is repeated. I am truly sorry that I am under the necessity of opposing your will in anything, my mother," said Ann in a lower tone, " but I cannot change—it is impossible."

" I have already told you—the matter has been settled. I have accepted Anthony Maddock as your future husband, and, as your mother, there is no doubt about my authority," said the mother, her face reddening with anger. " Now, go to your room, and in its loneliness learn to practise a more amiable and obedient spirit. Do you hear me ? "

"Yes, very well, and am prepared to obey you in everything that is reasonable, but never will I marry a man whom I loathe with all my heart," said the girl, walking quietly out of the room and leaving her mother alone, her mind thrown into a state of utter hopelessness by the disobedience of her daughter.

"What am I to do," she thought. "I have given my word, and more, the arrangements are made, and after all the trouble to abandon them as worthless to suit the humour of a mad and foolish girl is out of the question. Perhaps I had better leave the matter in Maddock's hands. If he joins we shall have a better chance." She remained in the room for a long time endeavouring to devise some scheme by which to secure her purpose, but her meditations were disturbed by one of the servant maids bringing a sealed packet, which, she said, she found carefully hidden in the rafter of Cae'rynwch. Mrs. Thomas hastily broke the seal, and found that it was a love song from the thatcher to her daughter. Will Hopkin's name was attached to it. It was as follows :—

> " Myfi sydd fachgen ieuanc ffol,
>   Yn caru'n ol fy ffansi ;
>   Fi yn bugeilio'r gwenith gwyn,
>   Tra arall yn ei fedi ;
>   O, pa'm na ddeui ar fy ol,
>   Ryw ddydd ar ol eu gilydd ?
>   Waith 'rwy'n dy wel'd, y feinir fach,
>   Yn lanach, lanach beunydd.
>
> " O ! glanach, glanach wyt bob dydd,
>   Neu fi sy' a'm ffydd yn ffolach ;
>   Er mwyn y Gwr a wnaeth dy wedd,
>   Gwna im' drugaredd bellach ;
>   O ! cwyd dy ben, gwel acw draw,
>   Rho i mi'th law, Ann dirion,
>   Waith yn dy fynwes bert ei thro
>   Mae allwedd clô fy nghalon.

" Mi godais heddyw gyda'r wawr,
   Gan frysio'n fawr fy lludded,
Fel cawn gusanu llûn dy droed,
   Fu 'rhyd y coed yn cerdded ;
O, cwyd fy mhen o'r galar maith,
   A serchus iaith gwarineb,
Waith mwy na'r byd i'r mab a'th gâr
   Yw golwg ar dy wyneb.

" Tra byddo dw'r y mor yn hallt,
   Tra byddo 'ngwallt yn tyfu,
A thra bo calon yn fy mron,
   Mi fydda'n ffyddlon i ti.
O, dywed i mi'r gwir heb gêl,
   Rho im' dan sêl atebion,
P'un ai myfi neu arall, Ann,
   Sydd oreu gan dy galon."

Mrs. Thomas was much concerned as to whether the song was hidden by Will before he left the place, or was he still hiding in the neighbourhood. She rang a small bell that was on the table, and asked Anthony to join her. It was a great satisfaction to the selfish and cruel mother —after carrying out her purpose with her daughter and relating what had taken place—that Anthony received the news without any apparent concern.

" I was prepared to receive, and expected something like it," said he quietly. Let the matter rest for a time. I feel quite easy and confident after having had your consent, and your influence in my favour. It requires only discretion and patience to get Ann to accept my hand readily. She is still young—and so beautiful ! Such a treasure is not to be had without trouble, and the greater the difficulty to secure an object the greater will be the enjoyment when it is secured."

"But it's her rebellion against my will that kills me, Mr. Maddock—her selfishness in refusing you when I considered it an honour that so respectable an applicant sought her hand. Is such conduct to be tolerated by me —her mother? And further, what is your opinion of this?" handing him the song.

Maddock took the paper and read it hastily, with a degree of impatience that was perceptible.

"It is from Will Hopkin," said he. "How came it into your hands?"

"Ann Llewellyn, the servant, found it hidden in the rafter of Cae'rynwch when returning from milking the cows this morning."

"Then I advise you to keep it private from Ann. And, by the way, it would be worth our while to win Ann Llewellyn over to our side. She is a sensible and cunning girl, and her young mistress appears to have considerable confidence in her. I will speak to her if I have a chance before leaving to-day. Let everything rest for the present. I will take care not to press Ann too much for an answer and tire her by taking too much notice of her, and in time her dislike may leave her and she may come to approve of your choice of a life partner for her."

"Well, let matters remain so. We leave them where they are for the present," said the mother.

CHAPTER XIV.

THE HERMIT.

BETWEEN the rivers Garw-wy and Llyfnwy stands a mountain, or rather a chain of high hills, called Moelgilliau. Looking upon their bare and rocky tops, we are bound to admit the name is truly descriptive of them. These hills, in olden time, were the stronghold of a gang of robbers, who were the terror of the country, and were known as the " Red Goblins." Many robberies had been perpetrated by them on the Moelgilliau hills, where they felt themselves safe and at home ; and every effort to get at them once they were within their refuge was fruitless. But the country became enlightened, and the robbers had to give way to civilisation, and had disappeared long before the days of the Maid of Cefn Ydfa, but many a long evening was spent in winter time in relating stories of their incredible bravery and cunning tricks.

Although the robbers had left the place for ages, it was seldom that anybody was to be seen in the neighbourhood of Moelgilliau. The place was regarded by the farmers as too poor to be cultivated ; and the fox and other wild animals found it, consequently, a safe shelter for the enjoyment of their freedom. On the side of one of the hills there was a large cave, known as the " Giant's Cave," and we are assured by tradition that the chief of the robbers lived in it. The name of this cave was a terror to all the children of Llangynwyd, especially when

threatened to be sent thither for offences committed.
The name and traditions were so romantic and frightful
that it was as terrible to the inhabitants as the Valley of
the Shadow of Death.   This cave was occupied in the
time of the Maid of Cefn Ydfa by an old man, who loved
the romantic solitude of the place better than the turmoil
of society.   What induced him to lead such a life, and
who he was, caused much discussion among the inhabitants of Llangynwyd.   He was always known as the
" Hermit of Moelgilliau."   Many strange stories were
told of him, which were only the fruit of human imagination.   Some thought he was a conjurer, and that he
was associated with the " Evil One."   He held no
fellowship with anybody, but if he met a person when on
his travels, he would talk freely and cheerfully, unless
he was questioned about himself.   He would answer no
inquiry about himself.   He had reached old age, and
had a patriarchal and dignified appearance.   His hair
fell in silvery ringlets over his shoulders, and his white
locks were adorned with gold and silver rings.   His
breast was covered with a thick beard, the greyness of
which proved that he received drops of the hoary
showers of the banks of the Jordan.

*   *   *   *   *   *   *   *

As we observed, Bess, Ann's mare, was waiting for Will
Hopkin as he came out of the cell in which he had been
confined.   Swiftly mounting, with a hurried farewell, he
rode off, leaving his sweetheart in tears.   He pursued his
journey as fast as the animal could carry him, and when
the dawn broke he had reached the wilderness of Moelgilliau.   There he dismounted, and, throwing the reins on
the neck of the mare, turned her face towards home.   He
thought of going into Carmarthenshire.   It was a lovely

May morning. The early breeze played its tender melodies upon the harmonious leaves of the forest, and the birds carolled their morning hymn from the branches. The unfortunate young bard looked back with longing eyes towards the dear home of his childhood, where he had spent the happiest days of his life, and which he was obliged to leave on account of his great love for the comely maid of Cefn Ydfa. He sat on a stone, and covered his face with his hands. It was no wonder that his heart was swelling. Whilst in that condition he heard a harsh voice address him from behind, and, springing to his feet, he turned and saw a tall old man of patriarchal appearance standing beside him.

" Who are you ? " Will asked respectfully.

" That is of very little importance to you, young man," answered the old man in a severe tone. " But what do you want here ? "

" I am on my way to Carmarthenshire."

" Where do you come from ? "

" From Llangynwyd."

" It does not appear as if you know the way over these hills ? "

" No, I have never been this way before."

" I know that, for you are fully half a mile from the right road. But you look tired, and must be hungry. Come with me to the cave, that you may have food and rest. It may revive your wearied and troubled spirit."

Will accepted the kind invitation with thanks, for he felt himself tired and weak, not having tasted food since the day before. They soon reached the mouth of the cave. The young bard was struck with wonder at the sight before him. In one corner of the cave there was a small chair, roughly made of wood ; whilst in the middle was a great stone, which served as a table, and was supported by two pillars of stone. On one end of the table was a big roll of manuscripts, which Will thought contained some important matter. On the other end were various herbs and roast meat. Suspended by wooden hooks from the roof were salted pieces of the swine of the forest, which had been hunted by the hermit. Neither were the bow and the basket of arrows wanting. After Will had rested on the small stool, Morgan (for that was the hermit's name) brought roast meat, and bread of his own making, and placed them before him.

Under other circumstances it would have been useless for Will to attempt to satisfy his appetite in so piggish and disorderly a place ; but as he was tired and hungry, he enjoyed his food immensely. When he had done justice to the dainties before him, Morgan began to catechise him about his past life, and soon learned that he was a fugitive on account of his love for the Maid of Cefn Ydfa.

" My son," said the hermit tenderly, " I fear you will not be safe if you succeed in reaching Carmarthenshire from your revengeful and cunning enemies. I like your appearance, and sympathise with you ; and you may remain here, if you like, my companion in this lonely old cave. You would be perfectly safe, and if anyone came in search of you, there is here a private chamber, in which you may hide, and I defy anybody to find you. You are fully welcome to everything you can see."

" But, father, suppose it becomes known that I am hiding here ? You will stand in as much danger as me ? "

" Leave that to me. I do not believe that any of them could muster enough courage to come here."

" I am not so sure of that, for there is scarcely anything too difficult or too despicable for Maddock and his son to do in order to accomplish their evil purposes."

Instantly, like a lightning flash, Morgan's countenance changed upon Will naming Maddock and his son, and fiery darts flashed from his eyes. He bent his head towards the ground, and appeared as if his feelings had been so much moved that he could not control them for a time. Will was afraid that he had said something to wound the old man, and said no more. Morgan remained in the same condition for a considerable time, and every minute seemed to Will as long as an hour. At last, Morgan lifted his head, and looking straight at Will, asked :

" Who do you say are your enemies ? "

" William Maddock, occupier and owner of Cwmyrisgla, and his son Anthony."

" I don't suppose that she cares for him ? "

" No. But every effort is made to induce her to accept him ; and the schemes for that purpose are not few, and they are at work to secure their object. William Maddock is one of the trustees appointed by her father till she comes of age, and he boasts that he can disinherit her of the estate of her forefathers."

The hermit uttered not a word, but bent his head between his knees, muttering, " Can the Ethiopian change his skin, or the leopard his spots ? " He raised his head suddenly, and said, " I will see—I may be able to do something for you and your beautiful Ann. Don't be disheartened nor give way to fear because of the knaves. No, it is not in the power of Maddock to disinherit her of her estate, which falls lawfully from her forefathers, the Thomases. But, my son, you must remain with me for a time ; and in the meantime I will level the difficulties, and hope to be able to change the counsel of Ahithophel into foolishness."

Will was filled with wonder at the language of the old hermit. What was the old man ? Did he intend invoking satanic influence to help him in the work he had promised to do ?

Will almost feared his companion by this time, but after pulling himself together and looking at the old man, there was something majestic about his appearance. His high and broad forehead indicated that he was a person of more than ordinary intellectual abilities ; and there was a tenderness in his eyes, sharp as they were, that made Will regard him with admiration, and induced him to place confidence in his new friend. In the course of that afternoon, as he felt tired, Will slept for hours ; and he was awakened from his sleep by the voice of Morgan as if in conversation with somebody. When Will opened his eyes, to his surprise, there was no one to be seen except Morgan, who was so deeply engaged with a large manuscript that was open before him that he paid no attention to anything else. Will did not move, but watched the movements of Morgan very carefully. At last, after a long examination of the old manuscript, Morgan leaned back against the wall and closed his eyes. After drawing his hand heavily over his forehead, Will heard him say aloud, " He it is, there is no doubt—at his old tricks again—but it will be better for him to stop. All the writings are safe with me."

CHAPTER XV.

"YOU wish to see me," said Mrs. Thomas, of Cefn Ydfa, one morning, about three weeks after the escape of Will Hopkin, as she entered the parlour of William Maddock, at Cwmyrisgla.

"Yes. I have important news for you, which will give, as I believe, as much pleasure to you as it gave to me. I have just received a newspaper, which contains an account of one of the most fearful shipwrecks I have ever read. It appears to have been a ship carrying emigrants to America, and there were some hundreds on board, who lost their lives, all but seven. Among the lost there is the name of William Hopkin, with the remark that he was a Welshman from Glamorganshire, and there is no doubt in my mind that he was your old tormentor Will, son of Hopkin Thomas. I have heard from several that he informed his friends that he would like to emigrate to America, in order to make his fortune, and it is very likely that what has taken place lately led him to put his purpose in practice, and I believe that he will give us no more trouble."

"But, Mr. Maddock, we are not to suppose that he was the only William Hopkin in Glamorgan. Indeed, I question whether he was possessed of sufficient courage to undertake such a dangerous voyage. And, further, where did he get the money to pay for his passage over the sea?"

" Well, Mrs. Thomas, there is not the least doubt in my mind that he is the man. And now, the poor and low thatcher is far enough, and we need not fear his passing our path again."

" Then there is nothing to prevent the marriage taking place at once, only the consent of Ann."

" True ; and we will have the matter over so soon as it is possible."

" But what if she continues obstinate ? "

" I will see her personally this afternoon," said Maddock. " Don't say a word about the shipwreck. I will inform her, and if she doubts it I will show her the name in the paper, that she may see it."

" It shall be so, then," said Mrs. Thomas, " and now I wish you good morning."

" Same to you."

Mrs. Thomas returned to Cefn Ydfa.

It was then the age of the ballad singer in every fair. There was not, perhaps, more than one newspaper taken in six or seven parishes, and the medium for the circulation of news was the ballad singer ; and when some mournful calamity happened it was made into rhyme, in the form of a song, and sung about the streets : and it was painted in the most frightful colours in order to sell. Neither was the news always reliable, for when the ballad market was slow, news was manufactured and sold by the hundred for a penny a piece. Such was the darkness and ignorance of the people of Glamorgan in the time of which we write.

Jack William Harry, the ballad singer, was a regular visitor at Llangynwyd, and his voice echoed through the streets when on his journeys ; and when the inhabitants heard his coarse voice they would crowd about him to hear the news.

The afternoon of Thursday that Maddock informed Mrs. Thomas, of Cefn Ydfa, of what he had read in the newspaper, Jack's unmusical voice could be heard singing his new ballad in the village of Llangynwyd. He was welcomed, of course, by the populace with astonished eyes, who surrounded him to hear his story.

"A ballad about a fearful shipwreck it is, my friends, that happened at sea about three weeks ago. The ship was full of passengers on their way to America, and it was wrecked in a terrible storm in the Bay of Biscay. The following are the names of the lost." He went through the lists, and when he came upon a certain name there was a movement among the crowd, whilst an occasional sigh was heard. One would exclaim, ' ' Poor fellow ! " And another, " Pity the poor widow, his mother.' That name was " William Hopkin, a Welshman, from Glamorgan."

There was no doubt in their minds that it was Will Hopkin, the thatcher, and it was not long before the news ran like wildfire through the neighbourhood ; and it is easier to imagine than describe the effect it had upon his aged mother. She felt that all the pleasures of life had been taken away by the death of her dear son. Her grief was too great for tears. All she said was :—" Oh, Will, my dear boy! Oh, that I had died instead of thee ! "

The news had not reached the ears of the Maid of Cefn Ydfa, when Maddock and his son made their appearance in accordance with the promise of William Maddock to Mrs. Thomas in the morning. The three shut themselves in the parlour, and remained in conference a long time before Ann was summoned to join them. At last, as she expected, the request came to go into the parlour.

" Well, Miss Thomas," said William Maddock as she entered the room, " a hard and difficult duty has been imposed upon me to perform, but I feel a special obligation to discharge it. I beg of you to keep as calm as possible."

" Speak out, I am ready," said Ann.

" We should speak with caution when announcing unfortunate accidents, especially to such as bear intimate relations to them. A fearful shipwreck has taken place lately, in which all passengers and hands were lost except seven, and in the list of passengers on board is the name of one whom we knew."

" Speak out, who was he ? " asked Ann impatiently.

" The ship was on her voyage to America, and when in the Bay of Biscay she sank, and among the unfortunate passengers was William Hopkin, the thatcher."

The broken-hearted maid said not a word, but bowed her head and covered her face with her hands, struggling to check the sighs that rose from her breast ; but, notwithstanding all her efforts, the soul uttered its distress in its own language. How Maddock came to know the heartrending news she did not know ; but she feared it was too true to harbour any hope of its falsity.

" Prove it to me. Let me see your proof of the truth of the story," she said at last, feebly.

" Here is an official report of the shipwreck, with the names of the passengers on board of the unfortunate ship," said Maddock, whilst spreading the newspaper before her.

She looked at it, and devoured silently every word

until she came to the name of William Hopkin. She returned the paper to Maddock, who remarked :—

" Now, Miss Thomas, are you satisfied that what I stated is true ? "

" Leave me, leave me in peace," she cried. A violent tremor shook her frame, a strange feeling of light-headedness came over her, and with closed eyes she swayed helplessly to and fro, Anthony barely saving her from a fall as he stepped forward and caught her unconscious form in his arms. She was carried to her room, and the family doctor was soon by her side, but all his efforts to restore her were unavailing for some time. She showed no sign of life.

" There is grave danger," said the doctor to her mother, who stood close by ; and at his request another doctor was sent for, who arrived in about an hour. They did all in their power to restore her to consciousness, but to no purpose. There seemed no sign of life—no movement or any stir in the quiet countenance to afford the frightened spectators a grain of hope. A painful silence reigned for a time, and the first to break it was her mother.

" Oh, my Ann ! my dear child ! " she said in a sorrowful voice.

" Don't give way too soon. She may be spared to you yet," said Dr. Griffiths.

The two doctors retired to the next room for consultation.

" Tell me, Griffiths, what am I to do ; I feel almost distracted ? " said Dr. Jones seriously.

" She cannot live in her present condition more than three hours ; and, whatever may be the consequences you have done the only thing to save her life. Give her this as soon as she comes to herself, if she does," said he, handing a folded paper containing a medical powder. " I am bound to go ; as I am wanted elsewhere." He left, and Dr. Jones went into the room where lay the Maid of Cefn Ydfa still in a state of unconsciousness.

Before the morning a heavy sigh passed her lips, and shortly afterwards she opened her eyes.

" Thank heaven, there is hope yet," said the old doctor.

He administered the medicine given him by Dr. Griffiths, and she became so much better, that he was able to leave with strict instructions to watch her carefully, and not to disturb her in any way.

He visited her again early in the afternoon, and announced that all danger was over, and that she required only rest and quiet in order to restore her to her usual health. His instructions were carried out to the letter, and care was taken to give her all she wanted. She kept her room for about a week, when the doctor ordered her to take a turn now and then in the open air. She was very glad of the arrangement, and often went out to the fields.

One day, when returning from a walk, she saw a tall old woman coming towards her, whom she recognised as the old gipsy who had told her that the future would be an unhappy one. In order to avoid her she turned from the path, but when the old woman came opposite her she stretched out her attenuated arm, speaking in plaintive voice. " Fair lady, your troubles are only beginning ! " She said no more, and went her way. Ann's heart was pierced by the dolorous prophecy and wailing voice of the woman. " Is it truly to be so ? " she thought.

CHAPTER XVI.

WILLIAM MADDOCK was a man governed by devilish principles, and if ever anyone sold himself to the evil one it was he. He had been guilty of the blackest crimes, and by his dishonesty and scheming had become possessed of great property, so much so that no one knew what he was worth. His neighbours placed very little confidence in him. They feared him as the mouse fears the cat, and the respect and homage paid was mere pretence and hypocrisy. He was a cunningly bad man, and his cunning proved useful to him on many occasions. Although it might be supposed that the wealthy owner of Cwmyrisgla was a happy man, yet he was the last in the district to be possessed of that valuable pearl.

In about a week after the news of the shipwreck and the drowning of Will Hopkin had arrived, William Maddock and his son Anthony sat in a large room, the window of which faced the fertile land before them towards the west.

" Now," said the father, " there is no time to be lost. Every moment is more valuable than gold. We must have the marriage over at once."

" But she is not willing."

" She must be forced to be willing. She must be compelled to submit, and that before long, or the bird will be beyond our reach. You know what I mean without further explanation."

" I know very well what you have in view, father, and as far as I know, it would be quite as well for me, and for her, that matters may be left where they are for the present."

" You simpleton," said the father, " do you wish to throw away such a golden chance ? No, it must take place, whatever be the consequences."

The son walked across the room patiently and looked through the window. In the distance he saw a tall old man of singular appearance making his way toward the house. There was something about him that roused the curiosity of Anthony Maddock, and he watched his progress with interest. As he was entering the field before the house he drew the attention of his father to him, and asked who might the old man be.

Maddock went at once to the window and looked out, and in a moment all his courage and self-possession left him. There was something in the appearance of the stranger which had a disagreeable effect upon him and his son heard him say, "True, it is he, although I thought he had been dead many years. Great heaven, help me ! " With this a heavy knock was heard at the front door, and one of the servants went to open it. The maid was a little frightened at the strange appearance of the visitor, especially when he asked in an authoritative voice—

" Does William Maddock live here ? "

The maid did not reply at once, and appeared in doubt what to say.

" Tell me, girl, is this the residence of William Maddock, the lawyer ? "

" Yes, this is where Mr. Maddock lives."

"Why not answer at once? Where is he? I must see him at once."

"But your name, if you please, sir?"

"Don't give yourself any trouble, but tell me where he is."

"In the front parlour, sir."

"Well, I will thank you to show me the way."

Maddock was within hearing of the conversation between the old man and the girl, and every member of his body trembled when he heard the sound of his steps approaching the door of the room. The stranger opened the door without any ceremony and walked straight towards Maddock, before whom he stood.

"William," said he, "could you not act more worthily of a reasonable being? Have you not yet learned to do unto others what you would like others to do to you?"

"What have I done to the contrary? Do I not always endeavour to do so? Have you ever seen anything different in my conduct?"

"No, you have been careful to be honest in your dealings with me at all times, but there are no thanks due to you for it, for you know how——"

"Hush, Morgan, for heaven's sake. I beg of you. Not another word on the matter. I place myself entirely in your hands, and will become your servant, ready to obey the smallest command, only that you keep the secret."

"Not a minute longer unless you satisfy me that you will not further persecute Will, son of Hopkin Thomas. I have recently found out that you, with your wily son, have been endeavouring to get the innocent young man out of the way in order that you may fulfil your wicked purpose and secure to yourselves the wealth of Cefn Ydfa. I now inform you that the young fellow returned to the neighbourhood this afternoon, and remember that if I hear further complaints of your conduct I will see that you will have your full deserts."

With a threatening look at Maddock, which nearly made him faint, Morgan left the room.

William Maddock did not know what to do. Will Hopkin was still alive, and all his plans were thwarted. He was as much afraid of Morgan as of death itself. It was evident that Will had informed the hermit of everything and secured his sympathy, and hence Maddock's fear.

" Everything is all up with us. It is useless for you to secure the Maid of Cefn Ydfa for a wife," said Maddock in a despairing tone to his son.

" Are we to be diverted from our purpose by the nonsense of this mad hermit ? "

" Little do you know who he is, my boy, and what is in his power to do to me. I dare not trifle with him."

" Well, if it is he alone who stands in our way we may devise some means to remove him."

" That is our only chance of success."

" Leave that to me," said the son. "A more hopeful view of things may yet appear."

Upon this one of the servants entered the room and handed a small piece of paper to Anthony Maddock, upon which was written—

" Sir,—Contrary to our expectations, Will Hopkin is alive and just returned from his place of concealment, and he has been seen near Cefn Ydfa speaking to Ann for some time. He returned in the company of a tall old man of strange appearance, who seemed to be very fond of him. We must be on our guard. There is no time to be lost."

CHAPTER XVII.

WILL HOPKIN ORDERED NOT TO GO NEAR CEFN YDFA.—
ANN CONFINED TO HER CHAMBER.

WILL HOPKIN enjoyed a few weeks' rest and quiet
after he returned from his old friend Morgan,
the hermit. He often visited Cefn Ydfa, the
house of his beloved, and thought that the worst was
over, and mentioned it one night to Ann.

"No," was the answer. "You don't understand the
two Maddocks as well as I do, and you may depend upon
it that they are not going to abandon their purpose so
easily as you think. I am afraid that they have a new
scheme on hand, which they are about putting in force."

"What makes you think so, my dear?" Will gently
asked.

Because William Maddock and his odious son visit my
mother too often to please me."

The next day dawned a beautiful morning in May.
The songs of the winged choirs, accompanied by the
murmur of the crystal brook which meandered through
the plain, formed a pleasing and appropriate concert,
whilst the hills around reflected the sun's rays, which
shone from a clear sky. Will Hopkin sat under the
shadow of a broad oak, with closed eyes and drooping
head, as if he had been overcome by a sudden and unexpected calamity, whilst he pressed a letter closely in
his right hand. How long he remained in that position
he did not know; and at last, the load being too heavy,

and paralysing his brain, he opened his hand, and looked with burning eyes on the lines that had caused him so much trouble :—

" Sir,—Mrs. Thomas, of Cefn Ydfa, requests me to inform you that the next time you are seen about Cefn Ydfa you will be arrested on suspicion that you are bent upon some unlawful purpose. I am,—William Maddock."

The first reading of the foregoing lines caused the tears to flow over his youthful cheeks, and after reading them over several times, they only increased his affliction and trouble. They, by their notice, prohibited him from ever again having the pleasure of seeing the face of his fair sweetheart. She was never again to rest her head on his breast, or he to embrace her lovely form !

" My Ann, my lovely Ann, is it to be so ? Is it my fate to be thus persecuted through life ? Am I to be surrounded by dangers wherever I go ? Are all those who have been kind to me going to turn their backs upon me in the day of my tribulation ? "

But at that moment, when his troubles seemed to have reached the extremity—when his future was in the balance—whether he would put an end to his life—a good angel whispered in his ear the words he had spoken many times to his beloved—" Wherever I am, and whatever my condition, I will always remember you, and will do nothing to cause you to be ashamed of him to whom you have given your heart." The image of his sweetheart stood before his eyes more lovely than the virgin loveliness of the fair lily of the valley. He rose, comforted by the thought, and with a kind of hopeless smile went on his way.

The Maid of Cefn Ydfa often boasted that she possessed the proud spirit which had characterised her forefathers, and, yet, notwithstanding all her courage and pride, there were times when she completely lost her self-possession, when the tears flowed unimpeded, whilst she breathed the name of him who had been prohibited from seeing her any more. The morning that Will Hopkin received Maddock's letter she was possessed by a painful fit of depression, which betokened some evil to take place. Her breathing was laboured and painful, and her heart was well nigh breaking. She threw her cloak carelessly over her, and went out to seek relief. She walked quietly towards a certain spot, near a wood to the east of the house, where she had spent many happy hours with Will.

" I will die first," she said, as she sat upon a big stone which was shaded by a large oak. " I will die first before I consent to be his wife."

" Did you speak, Ann ? I thought I heard your voice," said one whom she hated to the depths of her heart. " I am proud of the accident that brought me here."

" I hope it was accident that brought you here, Mr. Maddock, for I cannot permit any intentional inter-meddling whilst I am taking a private walk," said Ann in a stern voice.

" My dear Ann," he began in humble tones, but she stopped him in her impatience.

"Mr. Anthony Maddock, let us understand each other. I am willing to consider and act towards you as a gentleman, as long as you do not disturb me. But I cannot permit you, or anyone else to follow me and listen to what I may say in my loneliness," she said rising, and turning her face towards Cefn Ydfa, with a look of contempt upon her face.

" Oh, Ann, how cruelly you misjudge me," said Anthony Maddock sorrowfully. " As if I had ever, at any time, given occasion to hurt your feelings. Do I not abstain from pressing the chief desire of my heart— from using any authority to subdue your hatred towards me, and receive me as your future husband ? And, all for your sake, and to save you the anger of your mother, and not to interfere too much with your affairs ! Is that not deserving of some consideration at your hands ? "

" Scarcely," was her answer. " It is the duty of a gentleman to withdraw his request when he understands that he is not acceptable to the lady. And I do not consider that her rejection of him gives him a right to follow her wherever she goes and ask her for repayment of imaginary favours."

" You are cruel, Ann, but I'll bear this also ; although I might have revenge by concealing from you my message, which you ought to know ; but I have formed such an affection for you that I cannot give you up. I have news to tell you, and it was for that purpose that I sought you. All the necessary preparations for our marriage are made, and your mother has undertaken to reduce your obstinacy to her will ; but if you will not consent she has resolved, in virtue of her trusteeship, to disinherit you of the estate of Cefn Ydfa."

He had now revenge upon her to his satisfaction, for he noticed the blood rising in her face, whilst it disappeared the next moment, until she appeared as white as marble.

" Maddock," she said, after a short respite, "leave me,

I beseech you. Our meeting has lasted long enough, if not too long, and I wish to be alone."

He waved his hand significantly, but dared not disregard her request, and went away ill-pleased.

" I cannot believe," said Ann when alone, " without proof, and a clear proof. I cannot trust that wicked man. I cannot entertain the idea for a moment that my mother, of all persons, hard-hearted as she is, intends—if she has the power—to disinherit me of my righteous claim to the estate of Cefn Ydfa. I will continue to refuse Maddock in the face of everything. The whole thing is a cunningly devised scheme of their evil minds to induce me to accept him as my husband. But they may leave it alone. Will, Will, I shall prove worthy of you ! I shall be true to the end."

She hastily dried her tears, and walked quickly towards her home. After reaching the house she went to her room, where her mother was waiting for her.

" Where have you been so long ? " was her first question.

" I went as far as the wood, and happened to meet Mr. Anthony Maddock, and remained a longer time than I intended, talking with him."

Her mother asked no more questions ; she wished to know what had passed between her and Anthony, but she was possessed of sufficient prudence to conceal her anxiety from her daughter, and left the room. Ann spent the remainder of the day in her room, the privacy of which was more consonant with her feelings than anywhere else, and she was not in any way disturbed.

As evening came, she saw a young man approach her window cautiously, and place a small parcel on the sill and steal away. It was Will Hopkin. She tried to arrest his attention but failed, as she was afraid to call him lest her mother should hear. She opened the window, and picked up the parcel.

The Packman gave Ann a small box.

PAGE 109.

CHAPTER XVIII.

THE principality of Wales has undergone a complete change since the time of Will Hopkin and the Maid of Cefn Ydfa. The country was then swarming with small packmen, who travelled from place to place, and were, in distant and lonely places, the only means of communicating news, and were warmly received at the farmhouses. One day, shortly after the incidents related in the last chapter, one of the fraternity made his appearance before the kitchen door of Cefn Ydfa. He knocked at the door, which was opened by Mrs. Thomas herself, who, after seeing what he was, spoke cheerfully to him.

" Oh, is it you ? Please come in."

The packman followed her to the kitchen, where the two servant girls were engaged at their work. He was not long before he opened his pack and displayed his wares, which soon attracted the attention of the two girls, who regarded them with great interest. The mistress had gone to the parlour, and the girls and trader became more confidential, and Will Hopkin's name and that of their young mistress came on the board.

" I have heard," said the trader, " that a marriage is soon to take place—Mr. Anthony Maddock, of Cwmyrisgla, and your young mistress—is there any truth in it ? "

" It is likely, but no one has told us anything about it. But we know that Maddock and Anthony, his son, are frequent visitors here of late."

" That shows that the mother approves of the match ?"

" Yes, and she does all she can to persuade her daughter to accept the hand of young Maddock."

" H'm ! I suppose the heiress thinks highly of him ? "

" Not in the least, and I believe she has no affection for him, for I have heard her say that she dislikes and hates him from the bottom of her heart."

" So then force and not love will make Ann accept her husband ? "

" Oh, yes, for Will Hopkin she loves, and will remain his lover too, though she may be forced to marry Anthony Maddock."

" I have heard this morning that her mother had forbidden Will Hopkin to come near the house," said the trader in a low voice, " and that if he is seen about the premises he will be arrested as a criminal. Is there any truth in that ? "

" Yes, I am sorry to say. Old Maddock wrote to him the day before yesterday to that effect at the request of her mother, and Will has not been seen about here since. The matter has been kept a secret from her."

" I pity Will," said the packman. " But what is the reason that her mother is so much against him. He bears a good character, does he not ? "

" Nothing, but that he is a poor working man whilst Ann is a rich heiress and descended from an old and honourable family. Her mother felt that if she allowed them to associate together it would end in marriage, and she has consequently broken off any connection between her and the poor thatcher."

" And I have heard," said the other servant, coming nearer and bending her head towards him, " that William Maddock is one of her trustees, and that he has authority to disinherit her of the estate. But I cannot be positive, although it is said that he has threatened to use it if she does not yield to the wishes of her mother. There is something that has produced a great change in her lately."

" If Maddock is so much disliked by her I hope their purpose will fail, and that she may soon find a way of deliverance. I always looked upon Maddock as a gentleman, but by his continual attacks upon this young lady he has proved himself unworthy of the title. But time is going, my sweet girls, and although your company is pleasant I must leave you. Do you want to buy anything ? "

They bought a few small things, and as he was closing his pack the Maid of Cefn Ydfa came in.

" Why did you not inform me that the old man was here ? "

" Begging your pardon, mistress, we thought that your mother had informed you of his presence, for it was she who opened the door for him."

Ann suspected who he was and purchased a few things. She could scarcely prevent herself from speaking, but was afraid.

As the packman was leaving he gave the two girls a pair each of shoe buckles, which were in great request at the time, and gave Ann a small box.

Upon her receiving the parcel from his hand a careful observer might have noticed that her eyes filled with tears. She knew who the packman was. There standing before her was the chief object of her affections, but she dared not speak to him. She retired to her room, carrying the box with her. After reaching it, and satisfying herself that there was no one within sight or hearing, she opened it and found it contained a letter for her. The contents of the letter gave much ease to her troubled mind. It was as follows :—

"My dear, dear Aɪn —As I find no other means of seeing you and to assure you of my fidelity in the face of threats and dangers, I determined to visit the house in the character of a packman, and you see how I have succeeded. A few days ago I received a letter from the tricky knave Maddock prohibiting me from coming near Cefn Ydfa under the penalty of my being taken up as a vagabond. It is hard upon me, is it not ? To be prevented from seeing the greatest treasure I have upon earth—the spring of all my comforts ! Oh, my dear. how often my mind wanders towards your home and the places wherein we spent many happy hours, without any trouble to vex us, when the time passed so quickly and the time for separation came so soon—much too soon for us ! Time passed speedily—those happy times. But now, how different ! Such changes have taken place lately ! I dare not come near the house of my beloved, or to speak a word to her, or look at her bright face, and all because I am a poor working man. How cruel it is on their part to attempt to separate two who love each other so thoroughly. But they cannot prevent me from loving and admiring you. No, the mind can take many a flying visit to you. We have now only to hope against hope that there are better times for us in the future, and that every difficulty in our way shall be removed—that there is joy and gladness still waiting us, and, notwithstanding the wicked devices of our enemies, there is a store of comfort to us. Be courageous, and be assured that your poor admirer will be true to you whilst his heart continues to beat. I shall hide my letters in the future in the rafters of Cae'rynwch, where I hope to find an answer to this letter.—With a troubled heart, your unfortunate, but faithful,—" WILL."

The letter was read over and over again by Ann, and its contents were like " cold water to a thirsty soul.'

She took up her pen and wrote a few lines in reply, and as she finished there was a message that her mother wanted to see her. She obeyed at once, and, as she feared, the two Maddocks were closeted with her. The old question was again asked her, to which she replied—

"I ask nothing, but only claim what is fair and right —that is, leave me alone, and do not trouble yourselves about one who never will be anything but a friend to Anthony. I would never— if Anthony and I alone lived in the world—consent to become his wife. 1 will not marry a man I hate."

" But you are bound," her mother cried. " All the arrangements are made and completed, and I am determined that my plans shall not be turned aside on account of your obstinacy."

" If so, I wish to make it known to you that I would rather a thousand times leave my old home and its wealth than to give my consent to marry a man totally unworthy of my hand. If Maddock was possessed of the least particle of gentlemanliness and self-respect he would not attempt to force a fatherless girl to marry him against her will."

" Away from my sight," exclaimed her mother. " Go to your room, and in its solitude learn to honour your mother and show a more humble spirit."

" With pleasure, mother," said Ann, and went her way coolly.

" I do not know what to think of that girl's obstinate way. I must teach her to respect my behests better, otherwise she will cause me great trouble in the end."

" That is quite right," answered William Maddock, " and unless she is compelled to accept of a worthy applicant for her hand, and that soon, it is difficult to imagine what the consequences may be."

" You are right, quite right, Mr. Maddock, and I cannot much longer bear her obstinacy and opposition to my will. I will have a marriage settlement prepared at once, and then if she will not——"

" That will not do, begging your pardon, Mrs. Thomas. It will never do, for the report would go abroad that you are treating her cruelly. We must try to win her by caution and cunning to give her consent, and then all would come right."

Maddock drew his chair nearer Mrs. Thomas, and whispered something in her ear, and she listened, with her cheeks red with anger and her lips trembling, and when he had finished she cried out—

" The low and dirty scamp. Would I had the power to banish him from the country for life."

There was silence for a time, after which Mrs. Thomas asked Maddock what was his plan. Maddock bent his head to her ear, and continued whispering to her for some time. She listened to him, and her face underwent several changes. She turned pale more than once, as if she had been stabbed. She closed her eyes in contemplation, and then turned towards him and said—

" It is a fearful thing to kill an old man in cold blood, but I cannot see there is anything else to be done."

CHAPTER XIX.

THE PRISONER.

"MARY," said Mrs. Thomas, of Cefn Ydfa, to one of the servant maids the next morning, "don't let anyone go into Ann's room without letting me know."

"And, further, if you see a letter, or written paper addressed to her, bring it to me at once."

"I will."

The girl bowed her head in obedience to her mistress.

"Mind, and pay special attention to what I say, and you will be handsomely rewarded for any true service you may render to me."

Mrs. Thomas then left the room.

"What has she in hand now, I wonder?" the girl asked herself. "Does she want to make a spy of me, and thereby lead me to betray my young mistress to that odious Maddock and his son? If that is her purpose she will find out that she has made a great mistake." She then resumed her work.

Ann was not seen in the kitchen that morning, as usual, and the curiosity of the two servant maids was kindled by her absence. They could not account for this unusual conduct of hers, although their imagination guessed the cause.

About noon Mary was ordered to take dinner to her young mistress. She obeyed, and as she entered the room, Ann asked her if there was anyone with her. "No one," was the answer.

" Can I rely upon you keeping a secret ? "

" Yes ; any secret confided in me will be as safe as if in your own breast."

" I have always looked upon you as an honest girl, and have consequently much confidence in you. Will you put this letter in the hollow tree in Cae'rynwch ? Take care that no one sees you, or heaven only knows the consequences. Let it be done at nightfall."

" You may depend upon me, Miss, the confidence you place in me will be safe, and your wishes will be carried out to the letter, and as privately as possible."

" Depend upon it, I will remember you again."

The girl put the letter carefully in her bosom, and left the room.

At nightfall the faithful maid proceeded cautiously to the tree, and, taking the letter from her bosom, placed it carefully in the hollow pointed out to her. In about two hours afterwards a young man might have been seen approaching the place, and, after reaching the tree, putting his hand carefully in the hollow and taking out the letter and leaving another in its place. He then went away as cautiously as he came.

Next morning, as Mary took in breakfast to her young mistress, she was asked if she had been successful in her mission.

" Yes," was the reply.

" Had you time this morning to go and see if the letter had been taken away ? "

" No, I have not had a chance to go, but will take the first opportunity, and you shall know at dinner time."

" Very good, my dear friend," said Ann, with her eyes full of tears.

The servant then retired, leaving Ann in solitude. She was imprisoned within the walls of the house that was her own, and solely on account of her affection and fidelity to her dear Will. But she resolved to bear all rather than marry a man whom she disliked.

A little before midday the door was opened and Anthony Maddock walked in.

" Is not my penance to be over before our marriage ? Will not your cruelty give place to tenderness before then ? " said he, as he took a seat by the side of the unfortunate maid, whilst she moved further off lest even his clothes should touch her.

" Your penance is self-imposed and voluntary and my conduct has not been cruel," answered Ann, still moving as far from him as she could. " It is not too late for you to escape from both."

" Let us address each other by our Christian names— Ann and Anthony—as lovers always do."

" I do not consider that you have a right to call yourself my lover."

" Then you hate me—your future husband ? "

" Ask your own heart, if you have one, have I not had cause for it ? " said Ann.

" Oh, Ann ! Ann ! If you knew how greatly I love you," said Anthony, being wounded to the quick by her cool indifference towards him. " Truly I have proved the depth of my affection for you by agreeing to win you. Whatever the consequences may be, I will win your heart to love me yet."

" You must win me to respect you first, and that is totally beyond your power," she said. " You have darkened my life. You have touched the tenderest lines of my feelings in order to reduce me to obedience and give my hand to you in marriage, and yet you expect me to love you! It is unseemly and unreasonable. You have completely worn out my patience."

"See, I do not disturb you without an object in view. I have brought this small present to place at your feet," and handing her a small box full of the most beautfiul gems. "Don't you like them?"

"They look beautiful, and I must accept them I suppose. If that was your message to my room, may I beg of you to leave at once?" Anthony left without any further conversation.

"Proud girl," thought he, "it is not to be a fact. Were it not for the probability of my becoming owner of this place some day, with its wealth, it is true I would not bear her indifference and natred. However, when she is my wife, she will have to know who is master. She shall know that I will have perfect obedience, if nothing else."

As soon as Ann found herself alone, she threw away the box she had received from Anthony, and stood wildly, saying piteously, "Is it to be so in truth?" But she was prevented from saying more by the entrance of Mary the servant.

"Miss Thomas," said Mary, "the letter I placed in the hollow has been taken away, and another one left there in its place."

"Let me see it at once," she said anxiously.

The servant handed her the letter, which was in the handwriting of Will Hopkin. She read the contents with anxiety, and after she finished, said—her eyes brightening with delight—

"Oh, my dear Will, I shall be true to you. There is

no power in the world that would induce me to forget you and give my word to another."

"Would I be of further service to you?" asked Mary.

"Not now. I shall write a letter in the afternoon, if I have time, that you may put in the same place to-night, and for heaven's sake keep it a secret. Let no one know of the arrangement."

"Your mind may rest assured upon that point," said the faithful domestic, as she left the room.

Ann read the letter many times over, and her whole heart was fired by it. It contained the language of the soul of the young bard—his great affection and attachment for her. There was something within her which made her feel uneasy, and her soul yearned to be liberated from captivity, and to obtain its liberty. She could not sit quietly, but walked about the room, and looked out of the window. It was a lovely day, the lambs played in the fields adjoining in the plenitude of their freedom, whilst she was a prisoner. "Everything in nature enjoys its freedom—the sheep on the hillside, and the cattle in the meadow. The sound of freedom is in the singing of the birds, and the ripple of the rivulet speaks of liberty—but for me, I am a prisoner!" she mused. She opened the window, and was tempted to escape from her miserable prison. After a while she determined to call her mother, and ask permission to go out for a walk. The unnatural mother refused at first, but yielded afterwards on condition that she should not go beyond the neighbouring fields.

She walked slowly towards the spot where Will was taken prisoner by the press-gang on that anxious night. When she reached the place she jumped back frightened and were it not for an oak tree being near she would have fallen in consequence of seeing an object in the form of a woman, dressed in black, and coming out of the wood at the bottom of the field. She held to the tree whilst the strange object approached her by rapid strides. Grief and trouble had plainly left their marks upon the Maid of Ydfa—so weak was she that the sound of the breeze disturbed her. When the strange object came near, she remembered, to her terror, that it was the old gipsy who had told her before of her troubles.

"Fair lady, I am afraid that I have frightened you," said the old woman, "but you must excuse me for coming across you so suddenly and without notice ; I have a message for you—and for you only—too impo tant to be entrusted to anybody else, or to run the chance of seeing you in the house. I fear that your mother would not permit it. Are we safe here from being overheard ? "

"Certainly," answered Ann, whilst she trembled like an aspen leaf because of the fright that possessed her whilst hearing the strange words of the old woman.

"What I told you some time ago is becoming more likely every day to come to pass, and——"

She was stopped by a rustling in the copse close by, and the sound of footsteps coming towards them. They listened attentively in silence, and in two or three minutes a young man made his appearance.

CHAPTER XX.

"LEAVE me to my fate. I am bound to go. If I am seen here with you, woe is me."

"Halloo, Ann, listening to your fortune, is it?" said Anthony Maddock, for he was that young man.

"No, nothing of the kind," was the answer. "It is more than probable that my destiny is already sealed."

"You hellish fellow—you atrocious murderer," said the old gipsy, turning on young Maddock. "You are the true cause of this young lady's trouble and affliction, and as surely you will be the cause of her untimely death."

"Away with you, villain," shouted Maddock in a bitter voice, "or I will have you taken up for obtaining money under false pretences from the lady. Now, off with you at once."

"Villain, murderer, yes, unprincipled villain and murderer," responded the old woman. "I would a thousand times rather have a millstone tied to my neck and be thrown into the depths of the sea than stand in your shoes."

"Now, hold your peace, and be off, and don't let me see you about here again," said Maddock, lifting his hand threateningly over her head.

"I am going, and my constant prayer will be that your life shall always be under a terrible curse, and that you shall be pursued by a guilty conscience. Let your years be a series of troubles and disappointments, until your life becomes more of a load than a pleasure, owing to your cruel treatment of the unhappy maid of Cefn Ydfa, whom you, in concert with your father and her unnatural mother, are about to force to marry against her will."

As the last word left her lips she disappeared in the thicket, whilst Anthony and Ann stood as if struck speechless by the threatening words of the old woman.

"May I see you home ? Your mother wants to see you." He offered his arm, but she answered coldly, " No, I can walk without your help."

Not a word further passed between them. Ann's heart was burning too much f om the sorrows within for her tongue to speak, and could only give expression to her feelings by broken hearted sighs ; whilst, on the other hand, Anthony was oo angry to be able to speak.

He left Cefn Ydfa that afternoon. Early next morning, Mary, the servant, brought a letter to her young mistress from Will Hopkin from the hollow tree. Its contents comforted her very much.

Mary had to go from home that afternoon, and she entrusted the commission to place the letter in the hollow tree to Ann Llewellyn, the other servant.

Ann Llewellyn felt glad of the opportunity to carry out her evil designs. She had for some time felt jealous of Mary, her fellow servant, because of the confidence her young mistress placed in her, and now she saw an excellent chance of having revenge upon both, and resolved to carry it out.

William Maddock and Anthony, his son, were sitting in the parlour in deep conversation, when a stranger came towards the house and knocked at the door, which was opened at once by William Maddock. The stranger entered, and was shown into the parlour, and, after bowing to Anthony, said—" We have done the work."

" How did you succeed ? "

" Admirably. We came upon him when asleep. He is as dead as a nail."

" Very good. Did you secure the papers ? "

" Yes. These are all we could find."

' Excellent ! I had better pay you now. Reach forward your hand."

The stranger put forth his hand, and William Maddock counted fifty guineas into it.

" Thank you," said he, as he turned away.

" Well, Anthony," said the father, " our plans have been crowned with success so far. The old hermit has been removed out of the way. There was no chance of success whilst the old knave was alive. I feared many a time that the old fellow would let the cat out of the bag about our business ; but it is evident now that there was no need to fear."

" Nothing stands now between us and reaching the mark, except reducing her to obedience."

" That's all."

" Master, the servant girl of Cefn Ydfa wants to see you," said one of the domestics at the door.

" Show her in at once," said Maddock.

In two or three minutes Ann Llewellyn was in the room with th m.

" Begging your pardon, gentlemen, for disturbing you. I have something that would probably be of use to you."

"Of use to us, did you say? Speak out," said Anthony, astonished.

"Yes, of great advantage to you. But I may be interfering with a matter of no advantage to me."

"If you have anything to say which you think would be useful to us to know, you will be well paid for every service you may render us."

Ann handed him the letter which Mary had entrusted to her to put in the hollow tree that afternoon.

"Here it is again, father. Look over this. Will and she continue to correspond. A stop must be put to it, or our plans will be spoiled," said Anthony Maddock.

The father looked over the letter a second time, and thoroughly agreed with his son. Ann Llewellyn was rewarded for her service, and was cautioned to keep the matter private, and to bring every letter and every secret entrusted to her keeping to them; and that she would be handsomely rewarded for it. She promised to do so, and went off.

When about halfway between Cwmrisgla and Cefn Ydfa, whom should she meet but Will Hopkin, the bard.

"Halloo, Ann, where have you been this way?"

"To Godreuhen," was the untruthful answer.

"How is your young mistress now?"

"You may imagine that her condition is not a happy one."

"It is not, there is no doubt. Do the two Maddocks visit Cefn Ydfa frequently?"

"Yes, many times during the week."

"H'm! Do you know if my letters have reached Ann?"

Oh, yes, every one."

" I am glad to hear it.   But can I trust you with a secret that no one shall ever hear of it ? "

" You may trust anything to my care, and be easy in your mind that neither you nor her shall be betrayed by me."

" Then take this lette , and give it to your young mistress at once."

" I will.   I am certain to do it," was the answer, and away she went.

The heart of the deceitful Jezebel was fluttering with delight at the chance of putting her spiteful plans into operation.   The Maid of Cefn Ydfa never saw the letter, but Ann Llewellyn kept it until she could place it in the hands of Anthony Maddock.

CHAPTER XXI.

BITTER STORM.

"IS Mrs. Thomas at home ? " was the anxious inquiry of a gentleman at the door of Cefn Ydfa as one of the servants opened it.

" Yes," was the reply. " Will you please come in, sir. She will be here directly."

The gentleman was shown into the parlour, and took his seat until the arrival of Mrs. Thomas.

" Mr. Jones, how are you this long time ? " asked Mrs. Thomas, cheerfully, as she entered the room.

After shaking hands warmly the gentleman said—

" I have the marriage settlement of your daughter and Anthony Maddock. I expect Mr. Maddock and his father will be here shortly. He promised last night to be here to meet me at eleven o'clock this morning."

" All right, Mr. Maddock is always punctual."

As the words passed her lips the gentleman in question appeared at the door of the room.

" And you have arrived, Mr. Jones ? " said he, offering his hand to the strange gentleman.

" Yes, with the exception of the signatures of the parties to it."

" Very good. That will soon be done. My son Anthony will be here directly, and in the meantime Mrs. Thomas and I, as trustees of her daughter, will attach our names to it."

The document was spread on the table before them, and William Maddock and Mrs. Thomas signed their names to it. Anthony Maddock had joined them by this time, and put his name to the document.

" There," said the lawyer, for such was the strange gentleman, " there is nothing more wanted but the signature of your daughter and all will be over."

" Better then have her here at once."

The servant was sent to Ann requesting her immediate presence in the parlour. It was an anxious moment whilst waiting the arrival of the young lady. They soon heard her steps coming towards them, and the next moment she was in the room.

" Well, Miss Thomas," said the lawyer, " we want you to put your name to the document, if you please."

" I do not know what it is, and I am careful about what I put my name to, and I feel the same with regard to this. If I put my name to it I may have reason to regret it."

" Read the contents of the document to her, Mr. Jones, if you please," said her mother.

" Well, Miss Thomas, it is only fair and right that you should know what you are going to sign. It is a marriage contract between you and Mr. Anthony Maddock, and——
——" The old lawyer proceeded to read, but was stopped by Ann.

" There is no occasion for you to read any further. My determination has been made already. The contract is no good, for I will not sign it."

" But you are bound to do it," exclaimed her mother, " I am unchangeable in my determination to compel you to give your hand to a gentleman whom I consider worthy to receive that honour."

" Never—never—never ! " was the resolute answer.

" I am determined to humble you. I will make you sign. And now we are wasting valuable time, so put your name to the document."

" My mother, you of all should be the last to force me to marry a man whom I hate and despise. Consider that I am your child, your only child. Where is your motherly tenderness ? What has become of the affection that has always characterised you for me—gone ? Have you bred me up for your cruel amusement by seeing my misery and grief in being compelled to marry one whom I do not love ? Before ever I can sign a marriage contract with Anthony Maddock I mus ignore myself altogether. A thousand times would I rather welcome death in its greatest terrors—I would rather throw myself into the arms of the King of Terrors—than put my name to that document."

" And you are determined then to reject me ? " said Anthony Maddock, in a tone of disappointment.

" Yes, I shall never be a wife of yours ! The idea of such a thing is almost driving me mad. It is impossible. Nothing will change my resolve."

" Consider the matter for a moment. Be warned and advised in time, my dear girl."

" Don't torture me. Don't crush my brain with such talk Oh ! I feel the bitter flames of hatred towards you are burning in my breast when I look in the faces of your villainous father and yourself—filthy, fiendish, un-natural and heartless wretches that you are."

These impassioned words were spoken in a tone that expressed the storm that was passing through her bosom at the time. None of them dared ask her any more questions. She left the room and went to her own chamber, and there she laid on the floor, where her pale and wan face was washed with her tears.

After her departure from the parlour the small party remained silent for a while. After a short time the old lawyer observed—

" If you take my advice let matters remain as they are for a week or two, and in the meantime use every device to persuade her to sign the document voluntarily."

It was so agreed, and when on the point of separating, Ann Llewellyn, the servant maid, handed Mrs. Thomas a sealed letter, which, she said, she found in the cattle yard. Mrs. Thomas opened it, and it would be difficult to describe her anger when she found it was from the poor thatcher. Here it is :—

"My dear Prisoner,—I have your letter, and cannot find language suitable to express my delight at having heard from you. It was such comfort to my distressed mind to find that your love for the poor thatcher has not cooled, although a prisoner on his account. How can they treat such an angel so cruelly ? Oh, my beloved one, take heart, and remember that your Will will ever remain true.

" Tra byddo dw'r y mor yn hallt,
     A thra bo'i wallt yn tyfu,
   A thra bo calon yn ei fron,
     Fe fydd yn ffyddlon i ti !

" You can depend upon me, I shall remain faithful to you, and whether in want or plenty, trouble or prosperity, I cannot love another for ever.—This from your faithful
                              " WILL."

" So they are at it yet I see, notwithstanding our watchfulness over her. An end must be put to this correspondence, or it may lead to an escape some night, and that would be an everlasting disgrace to the name of the honourable family of Cefn Ydfa," said Mrs. Thomas.

" The sooner a stop is put to it the better. That a lady of such a high family should carry on a clandestine correspondence with such a contemptible brute is a disgrace to the family," answered William Maddock.

" I will manage it. She shall not see this letter, and I will give strict orders to take away every instrument that may enable her to write from her room, and will keep a more careful watch over her movements. And if I find that either of the maids carry letters from one to the other she shall leave the house at once. I will see to it this afternoon."

" Yes, it would be better to confine her within the walls of her chamber and prevent her having interviews of any kind outside the house," said William Maddock.

" I agree with your suggestion, and will give orders to that effect at once, and she shall have the chance of coming to her senses in her prison only, for there is nothing else to do with the obstinate creature."

The Maid of Cefn Ydfa sat in her room that afternoon, and the light of the small candle on the table shining upon her pale face showed that the hopeful cheerfulness which had characterised her had completely gone from her beautiful black eyes. Her hope had disappeared.

" Will, Will, you, and you only, are my comfort in my miserable condition," she murmured.

At this she heard the door opening, and, Ann Llewellyn coming into her room, without saying a word, took the candle from before her, and, gathering all the papers and writing materials together, went out with a satanic smile on her countenance.

" It makes no difference," whispered the unfortunate maid sadly. " If they imprison my body within these melancholy walls they cannot confine my mind or change my affections. I shall be true to you, oh my dear Will, whatever may happen."

She rose and walked across the room, pressing her hands to her burning forehead which frightened her.

" I am bound to be quiet ; I cannot afford to be ill," she said. " Merciful heaven, help me ! I must control myself."

Possibly her prayer was heard, for sleep came to ease her torments. She slept for hours, and when she awoke the sun's bright rays were cheering her sad room. She looked sorrowfully through the window. How beautiful the scene appeared—the tall trees, the broad meadows clothed in their green spring verdure. Far in the distance through the branches of the trees, the tower of the ancient parish church, within which rested her forefathers, might be seen, rising proudly, as if to kiss the clouds.

Soon her breakfast was brought to her.

" You may take it away," she said to the servant, " I shall not be able to take any of it."

The waiting maid was astonished, and stood, not knowing what to do. At last she said—

" There was no letter in the hollow tree to-day, Miss Thomas, and I have reason to think that Ann Llewellyn has seen some of the letters, and informed your mother that I was helping you to correspond privately with Will Hopkin."

" What has made you think so, Mary ? "

" Yesterday afternoon your mother told me to look for another place at the end of the week."

" I understand it now. Ann was here last night and

took away all writing materials from me. Good heavens ! What a treacherous viper we harboured in the house," exclaimed Ann.

" I am bound to leave you," said Mary, " or they will suspect me. If there is anything you would like Will to know you may rely upon my fidelity, notwithstanding their opposition."

" But I have no paper or anything to write upon."

" I will find paper for you by dinner time," said the faithful girl, as she left her afflicted young mistress.

CHAPTER XXII.

LOVE AS STRONG AS DEATH.

THE Maid of Cefn Ydfa remained a prisoner in her room, and, notwithstanding every effort to induce her to marry Maddock, she remained as firm as a rock in the face of all promises and threats. Writing materials were taken away from her room, it is true, and yet she was able to correspond with Will without their knowledge. Her only companion in her loneliness was a splendid cat. It is said that necessity is the mother of invention, and so it was with her,—when she had neither ink nor paper, she punctured the ears of the innocent creature, and wetted the point of a pin in its blood, and wrote on scraps of paper she found about the room. But this scheme of her's was discovered, and her companion was taken away from her.

Mary's week's notice was up, and the faithful girl had left the house, and her place was taken by the traitress Ann Llewellyn, who acted as spy for Maddock. Whatever she heard or saw was carried to him, until the condition of the unfortunate young lady was becoming more oppressive every day, and she often wished that death would put an end to he troubles. She had not received or heard anything from Will Hopkin for several days, and felt herself bordering on madness.

One day her attention was accidentally drawn to a bit of paper on a shelf in her room. She picked it up, and, opening one of the veins of her arm, she dipped the point of a pin in her blood in order to send a few lines to Will. This is what she wrote :—

"My dear Will,—Oh, your Ann is in great straits! This writing has been anointed with my tears, and written with the blood of my broken heart. But, although imprisoned, my love for you has never been shaken. No, you fill my heart ; and, when I have no other means, I use my own life blood to write to you! Oh, Will, dear, would I had one sight of your ruddy and amiable face—to rest on your bosom, and hear the beatings of the heart that is so fond of me once again! I would be willing to sacrifice all I possess to obtain it! Winds of heaven, be merciful, for I have no other way to send to my beloved, except upon your wings! Oh, take it safely to him who is so dear to my soul—the possessor of my heart! My condition is bordering upon madness! I cannot describe the torture of my mind to you! But I will die before I break the promise of fidelity which I swore to you, which is so sacred in my sight! I shall go to my grave in the spring of my life before I consent to their request! Be true, Will, to the maid whose heart bleeds for you!"

She opened the window, and cast the paper to the mercy of the winds.

That afternoon her mother paid her a visit, and endeavoured by promises and threats to persuade her to accept Maddock ; but it was of no use, she stuck unflinchingly to her resolution. Seeing that nothing would move her, Mrs. Thomas withdrew disappointed, and asked Anthony Maddock to see her. He refused at first, but yielded after much pressure, and entered the room. He found Miss Thomas sitting in a chair with the transparent tears rolling down her pale cheeks. He walked slowly towards her, and placed his hand tenderly on her

shoulder. If she had been stung by a serpent she could
not have been more suddenly alarmed. She jumped to
her feet, and, pointing to the door, said—

"Now—off—I cannot bear you here. I consider your
presence insulting to me."

"You are mistaken. I have no intention to insult you,
only respect and true——" "love" was on his lips, when
he was stopped by her.

"There, I have no wish to speak to you, and shall feel
glad to see you go back through the doorway, and leave
me in solitude! My feelings toward you remain un-
changed! I would a thousand times rather go to my
grave than become your wife!"

"Why? Why should you so dislike me, Ann? I can
claim an equal place with you in society as regards wealth
and position, and although I have no beauty to boast of,
yet there is nothing forbidding about me."

"True, Maddock; and if I had been left alone by your
father and yourself, I might be able to look upon you as a
friend, though there would be no sentiment in my breast
towards you. But I have been too much enlightened as
to your true character. I shall never forget the lesson
that has cost me so much to learn."

"H'm! So I understand that you will never promise
to marry me?"

"Never, so long as my heart continues to beat in my
bosom. If I were compelled to chose one of two things—
that is, marrying you or being thrown into a fiery furnace
—although the latter is awful to contemplate—yet, I
would meet the devouring flame with a smile on my
countenance before I would select the first! And now,
you have been here long enough, and heard my opinion
of you; so I shall be truly thankful if you go away."

Anthony turned away dispirited, without saying a word.

The hours passed away, and the sun sank below the horizon, and the queen of the heavens made her appearance on the verge of the starry sky. The Maid of Cefn Ydfa sat thoughtfully in her chamber, whilst—

> " Adgofion oes fel lli'
>   O hylif gwefrol,
>   Oe'nt drwy ei mynwes hi
>   Yn iasau ingol ;
>   Ei dagrau oe'nt yn dŷn
>   Dan folltau trystyd
>   Ond rhua'i bron bryd hyn
>   Fel mynydd tanllyd ! "

Her mind flew back to the past—to the happy days when Will and herself enjoyed liberty to associate together before any interloper had thrust himself between them, or any enemy had mixed wormwood with their cups. Whilst these recollections passed through her breast it is no wonder that her sighs were pitiful—for there was not the shadow of a hope that she would ever enjoy it again. With these feelings filling her mind she fell asleep. In her slumber she dreamt that she enjoyed the freedom as of old, and that Will stood before her looking as pleasant and attractive as ever. She thought that her enemies had gone away, leaving them to associate together without interruption. Excited by such thoughts, she arose joyfully to her feet and awoke ; but, oh ! only to find herself as much in captivity as ever !

A little before daybreak she thought she heard a beautiful voice singing, and rose and went towards the window : but, on looking, she could see no one nor hear the voice. When about leaving the window, she heard the sound

again, and realised it was Will Hopkin, and understood
they were verses he was in the habit of singing, namely—

" Glanach, glanach wyt bob dydd,
  Neu fi sy' â'm ffydd yn ffolach ;
Er mwyn y Gwr a wnaeth dy wedd,
  Gwna im' drugaredd bellach.
Mi godais heddyw gyda'r wawr,
  Gan frysio'n fawr fy lludded,
Fel cawn gusanu llun dy droed,
  Fu 'rhyd y coed yn cerdded."

Why he should have adopted such a strange method
she was at a loss to know.   He stood some distance away,
and how she could give him a sign that she was there
without disturbing the household she could not divine.
But what will not love do ?   She remembered there was
a secret method of removing the window, and imagine her
delight when she found the window loosening upon her
touching a spring.   In a few moments the two who
loved each other so dearly were clasped in a fond
embrace.

Both were so overcome with their feelings that they
could not speak for some time.

" Oh, my beloved, oh how glad I am to have you in my
arms once more !   I cannot tell you what I have suffered
at the thought of you being made a prisoner for loving one
so unworthy as me !   Did you get the letter I gave Ann
Llewellyn to give you, my beautiful girl ? "

The truth flashed upon her mind in a moment as to
how Will's letter had got into her mother's hands, and she
said, " No, Will, and no letter will ever reach me through
the hands of that deceitful jade."

" Why so ? "

" Because she acts as a spy for the two Maddocks and

my mother. But, dear Will, our meeting must end, however sweet it is. My time is short, and I must return ! What if my mother and the two Maddocks knew of our meeting ? I tremble at the thought of it."

One embrace close to his heart and a farewell kiss on her pale face, and they separated for the last time as lovers. Their next meeting would be under far different circumstances !

Ann crept back to her home as silently as she could. The morning breeze rustling the trees made her afraid, and gave wings to her trembling limbs ! What was it ? A dream, or did she hear someone near ? She believed it was a fancy of her own, and after reaching her room she thought no more of it. The load was too heavy and the cross too sharp upon the Maid of Cefn Ydfa to give attention to imaginary ideas without any substance in them.

CHAPTER XXIII.

THE TRAITOR VICTORIOUS.

" TRULY, Ann, I cannot bear any longer your rebellion against my will. Everything is ready, and I expect Anthony Maddock here to-morrow, and the marriage is to take place on Monday," said Mrs. Thomas, of Cefn Ydfa, to her daughter one lovely afternoon in May.

"Then I fear it will be a marriage without a bride unless Anthony finds one by the time," was the answer. "It is certain I shall never be a wife of his."

"Nonsense, child! I am determined to be obeyed or you will have to reap the fruit of your disobedience, for I will cause you to be incarcerated in the underground cell in which your Will—as you call the poor thatcher—was imprisoned, and you shall remain therein until you come back to your duty."

"I perform my duty now, and I will not be moved," replied Ann, in a determined voice.

"Out of my sight, ingrate. Now go," said her mother, "or I shall——," and in the excitement of the moment Mrs. Thomas rose her hand threateningly over the head of her daughter.

The consequence of Ann's refusal, as she expected, was that her mother put her threat into execution, and she found herself between the cold walls of the old underground cell. She was not to see or talk with anyone but

Ann Llewellyn and Anthony Maddock, who often visited her, much oftener than she wished. Every effort and scheme were used to influence her to marry Anthony, but all were unsuccessful. She appeared more determined than ever.

Three days after she was incarcerated in the cell a letter was brought to her by Ann Llewellyn, which she said was found in the hollow tree at Cae'rynwch that morning.

Ann looked with a degree of suspicion on the writing on the envelope, but she said not a word. She broke the seal and read the letter carefully, and on finishing it she cried out in a hopeless strain—

" Merciful heaven ! It is too much ! I cannot bear it ! " and she fainted. Before long she recovered, and appeared as if all consolation had left her for ever. She spoke very little, and when she did it was evident that she knew but little of what she said.

The letter, which she had read, was signed with the name of Will Hopkin, and its contents were as follows :—

" To Miss Thomas, Cefn Ydfa.—I take my pen to write the last letter you will receive from me. Considering the distance between our social condition and the many troubles you have suffered through your affection and fidelity to me, I, after thoughtful consideration, surrender all claims I have to your hand, and relieve you of any vow you have made to me. It is a great sacrifice to me, and I know that you will feel disappointed, but when life and honour are in the balance sentiment must give way, and there does not appear any other course open consistently with honesty and justice towards you. Heaven bless the fairest and dearest of Cambria's maidens ! Farewell ! —WILLIAM HOPKIN."

Of all the trials she had passed through this was the

She rushed towards him, placing her arms round his neck.

PAGE 143.

most bitter. Her Will—her sweetheart, her lover, the beloved of her heart, the only man on earth she loved—turning his back upon her in her distress! Was it possible?

A closer examination of the letter revealed one proof that Will had not written it, namely, that the personal pronoun " you " was used instead of " thee," which Will invariably used, but other points of the letter pointed to Will as the author.

A few hours later Anthony Maddock entered the cell. Ann was nearly distracted by this time.

" Oh, Ann, my beloved! listen to me for a minute. My heart has become so possessed by you that I cannot bear to see you in such captivity. I have done all I could to withdraw my affections from you, seeing that you dislike me so much," said Anthony. " I ask nothing from your hand, only the right to draw you to my bosom to protect you and comfort you as the chief object of my affections! I know that you do not love me, but you may forget the past in time and regard me differently and respect me as your tender and careful husband. Oh, say the word! Give me some reason to hope that I may yet have you the partner of my life and the wife of my heart."

" No, I cannot—I dare not. Don't ask me again."

" Ann, for heaven's sake, don't torment me any more! I cannot love anyone else, and my life will be a heavy load upon me to the end! Will you brighten my life, and make it a pleasure and delight by promising to marry me? "

" Maddock, I have told you before that I cannot marry any man whom I do not love."

" But Will has turned his back upon you and forgotten you, and has left the place, and no one knows where he

has gone to !   Ann, the idea of you being a prisoner within
the unhealthy walls of this chamber pierces my heart !
Oh, do promise to become my wife—only one sweet smile
upon me and I shall feel myself a happy man."

Ann felt that she had come to a crisis. It was pressing
upon her on all sides, and she must be guided by her
judgment. Her fate rested upon the answer ! She
closed her eyes in deep thought.   Will Hopkin, her lover,
had turned deceiver and forgotten her, and was she to remain true to one who had proved himself unworthy of her
and be kept in captivity for his sake ?   What was she to
do ?   At length she opened her eyes, and said—

" Anthony, you have succeeded in your object. Rather
than remain longer a prisoner I will bend to the will of my
mother, and will put my name to the marriage settlement."

" But what security have I, my dear Ann, for it ? "
asked Anthony, attempting to reach her hand, which she
withdrew hastily as if she feared his touch.

" The word of an honest maiden, Anthony. I can
easily excuse you, for you do not understand its value,"
she said bitterly. " Don't be afraid that I shall withdraw.
No, if I did it would be a witness of my sacrifice.   And
now, be good enough to leave me to myself."

The young man left the chamber with a smile of satisfaction upon his countenance. He went immediately in
search of Mrs. Thomas, and informed her of the success of
his pleading. The lawyer was sent for to complete the
contract, and he soon appeared. Ann was led from her
prison to the parlour to sign her name to the document.
Her heart was pierced when she saw the instrument on
the table, and she trembled so much that she could not

hold the pen. But when William Maddock saw that she appeared as if wishing to withdraw he took hold of her hand and forced her to attach her name.

CHAPTER XXIV.

THE week passed, and on the following Monday a large crowd of the inhabitants of Llangynwyd gathered about the porch of the old church in order to be eye-witnesses of the marriage of the Maid of Cefn Ydfa. The parties soon appeared, and Ann was led to the church by the father of the bridegroom. She looked pale and troubled, and in no way pleased—nay, far from it, as her deep sighs testified.

When ascending the narrow steps leading to the chancel wherein stood the altar, and seeing the old priest in his official robes waiting for them, Ann drew back, and, separating from William Maddock, cried out—

" No, no, I cannot. It is impossible."

Maddock turned round sharply, held her arm firmly, and remarked in a low even tone—

" It is too late to draw back now, my fair one. You must obey."

Notwithstanding her cries and prayer for liberty, he dragged her forward in the most cruel manner until she was in front of the altar, and in less than two minutes the son of Levi commenced reading the marriage service. He proceeded in the midst of the deepest silence, and when he took her hand to place it in that of Anthony she drew it back. He grasped it a second time and handed it to Anthony. The remainder of the ceremony was gone through without any further resistance from her, and the register was signed by the parties and the witnesses, and the bells were rung in honour of the wedding.

The Maid of Cefn Ydfa was led out of the sacred edifice by her husband—Anthony Maddock—her pale face and wan cheeks being wet with tears. She had scarcely sufficient strength left to enable her to lift one foot before the other.

Those who had assembled round the porch remained there still, and, upon the appearance of the wedding party, a tall young man and handsome to look upon, was seen making towards them. Taking no notice of anyone he came straight to the door of the church. When the bride saw him, utterly indifferent of the by-standers as well as her husband, she rushed towards him, placing her arms round his neck, and Will Hopkin, for it was he, found the Maid of Cefn Ydfa once more in his arms. Astonished silence prevailed for a while, neither the scoundrel William Maddock nor his son daring to separate the two who loved each other so greatly.

" Oh Will ! Will ! How could you act so cruelly towards me ? My heart is broken and every comfort is banished for ever," said the bride through her tears.

" Ann ! Ann ! my dear Ann ! my angel ! What does all this mean ? What do you mean ? "

" My Ann, if you please," said Anthony, indignantly, endeavouring to separate them. " Let her go, you villain ! Let her go, you impertinent vagabond ! What right have you to treat another man's wife in this manner ? "

But his attempt to separate them was useless. They appeared determined to cling together as long as they could.

Whilst this disturbance took place the attention of the crowd was directed to an object in the distance approaching them rapidly. When it came near the crowd opened and formed a lane through which rushed a woman who appeared mad. She was pale, and an unnatural and unearthly light flashed from her eyes. The bystanders were frightened. She paid no attention to any of them, and when she reached the spot where Will Hopkin, the Maid of Cefn Ydfa, and Anthony stood, she stretched her bare skeleton arm towards them, calling out, in a wailing voice, "Woe! Woe!! Woe!!!"

William Maddock rushed forward and endeavoured to take hold of the old gipsy, but too late, for as the last word escaped her lips she fell down in a fit, from which she never recovered.

With a fearful oath Maddock rushed at Will Hopkin, separating him from Ann, who was led to the carriage, notwithstanding all her efforts to the contrary, by Anthony, her husband, and in less than two minutes the carriage was driven off.

Will Hopkin, after the marriage of his beloved, resolved to leave his native place for ever, and that evening he silently left his cottage, fastening the door gently after him lest the noise should disturb the sleep of its only occupant. He had made his preparations and there was but one to whom he wished to bid farewell, and then he would be free to go. It was nearly two o'clock when he reached Cefn Ydfa. High in the cloudless heaven rode the moon and her modest rays made everything clear. He stood against an old stile—the spot where Ann and he had spent many a pleasant hour, whilst he had pictured their future home and the happiness of its occupants. That happy time he did not hope to enjoy again. He looked in the direction of the cell in which he was a prisoner that long-to-be-remembered night when the Maid disclosed the strength of her affection for him, and then turned his eyes to the room through whose window she came out to him, when he enjoyed her society for the last time ! No wonder that he cried ! Shedding tears was natural to him ! The blow was sudden and unexpected ! His simple and unsuspecting soul could not realise how things could so happen—why the most lovely and sweetest maiden under the sun should break all her vows which were so sacred in his sight ! Poor Will ! The contents of the cup were bitter. He then turned his attention to the expanse of country before him upon which the silvery rays of the cold full moon fell all around. Every hill and dale, every tree and flower, the small clear rivulet, with the cottage and its whitewashed porch, were indelibly impressed upon the tablets of his memory. Often in the course of his life was that night restored to him— the clear unclouded sky, with the moon on its bosom, the surrounding country, the homely cottage in the valley, the ancient church and tower, came so fresh to his memory that he saw them before him, and prayed for rest and peace from their presence ! Unfortunately for him, he possessed so retentive a memory that he could not forget anything. His heart was unchangeable.

With tears in his eyes he bade farewell to the place, turned away, and commenced his journey.

CHAPTER XXV.

THE DISTRACTED WOMAN.

Nol eistedd wrth y bwrdd,
Ymwylltiai'n fuan
Cyfodai, rhuthrai ffwrdd,
Gan waeddi allan, &c.

TWO years had passed since the marriage of the Maid of Cefn Ydfa and Anthony Maddock. To some the time had brought happiness and joy, but to Ann Maddock only additional misery and trouble. A stray silvery thread might be observed in the hair of her head. Her cheeks were pale worn and furrowed. But her outward changes were poor indications of the internal —the secret sorrow whose sword constantly pierced her heart until it bled in a constant stream. There was a wonderful difference between the maid of eighteen and the married woman of twenty-one. The joy and cheerfulness which formerly characterised her eyes had disappeared, never to return and their place taken by disappointment and grief.

After the marriage she and her husband went to live in a house midway between Cwmyrisgla and Cefn Ydfa, but she did not enjoy a moment's pleasure the whole time. In about a year after settling there she was taken ill with a severe fever, and it was feared that she would not recover. She lost all consciousness whilst ill, and called wildly upon Will Hopkin to come to her. She appeared sometimes to be in deep conversation with him, when suddenly he seemed to pass from the gentle hands that sought to detain him. Her mind was always attracted in one direction, like the needle to the pole.

After recovery, she refused to stay any longer in her husband's house, and returned to Cefn Ydfa.

It was evident that the fever had left an unfavourable effect upon her senses, and she often rushed out of the house singing :—

" Mae'm bys yn cyneu'n fflam
　　Mae'r fodrwy'n eirias ;
O ! ymaith a hi, mam—
　　Mae'n dân o gwmpas :
Ni pherthyn ddim i mi—
　　Nid wyf yn briod ;
Will Hopkin garaf fi,
　　Er maint fy nhrallod.

Och fi, fy mam, fy mam,
　　Yr oe'ch yn ynfyd,
Yn gwneyd a mi'r fath gam—
　　Yn difa'm bywyd ;
Chwi'm gwerth'soch wrth eich blys,
　　Ofnadwy gethern,
Mae cadwyn am fy mys
　　Mor boeth ag uffern !

Chwi wnaeth y tân, fy mam,
　　A phwy a'i chwythodd ?
'Rwy'n ysu yn y fflam—
　　Pwy fedr ei diffodd ?
Fy mam, mae'r fodrwy'n dan !
　　O, deuwch yma
A malwch hi mor fân
　　A llwch diddymdra !

> O, Will ! O Will ! un waith
> Dy wel'd a geisiaf ;
> Os sychu'm dagrau llaith,
> Yn foddlon trengaf."

Her movements were carefully watched by her mother, but notwithstanding all precautions, she often escaped from the house, and her pitiable cries were frequently heard in the neighbourhood— " Will, my dear Will ! where are you ? My dear, come to me ! No, you refuse ! See, oh see my affliction ! Look with pitying eye upon me ! Don't turn your back upon your Ann in her misery ! Oh, don't ! Listen to me singing your song," beginning to sing "Y Gwenith Gwyn," but before completing the first verse she would break into a hopeless fit of crying.

Her mother was beginning to repent her cruel treatment of her only daughter, and her conscience roared like a bear, but the repentance was too late. Ann's condition was getting worse and worse continually, and she would be heard in the silence of the night crying out in her room, " Will ! Oh, my dear Will ! "

Anthony, her husband, dared not come near her, and she often prayed that all the curses that a broken-hearted woman could invent might fall upon him, and in her frenzied state her curses upon her mother were something fearful. It was vain for the mother to try to console the daughter. She walked out in search of Will, she said, to the places where they usually met, the sight of which made the hopeless tears to flow copiously from her eyes ; and the hills which formerly echoed her mirth now only repeated her broken-hearted cries when calling out, " Will ! oh, my dear Will ! "

She was always followed in her walks by her mother, of whom she took no notice. Her mother prevailed upon her to vary her walks, so as to wean her mind from its sad condition, and to draw her attention to new scenes. But where true love exists it sees everywhere traces of the object of its affections. Day or night, in silence or solitude, in the midst of quarrels and noise, though time may throw the shadow of forgetfulness over many circumstances, yet it cannot efface those recollections that are dear and sacred to the heart, which, like the needle of the compass, trembles at the touch of the loadstone, and reverts to the direction of the pole, which is its natural attraction.

The doctor had informed the mother that the only hope of her recovery was to allow her to have her own way.

One cold morning her mother was much frightened on entering Ann's chamber to find her absent. An alarm was instantly raised, and all the domestics were sent in search of her, but every effort proved fruitless until late in the afternoon, when she was discovered in a deep ditch near the house, apparently dead. She was carried home, and the doctor was soon by her bedside. Signs of life shortly showed themselves, and by the skill of the doctor she was restored.

This accident had a disastrous effect upon her, and she was confined to her room by an illness which never left her. It was evident by this time that her life was quickly hastening to its end. The difficulty of breathing and a dry cough indicated that her days were numbered. She spoke little, and when she did it was about Will Hopkin. Will had not been seen in the neighbourhood since the day of the marriage, and nobody knew where he was or whether alive or dead.

One afternoon in the beginning of June the Maid of Cefn Ydfa rose suddenly in her bed, looking wildly about the room, as if she had seen something extraordinary.

" Did you see him ? " she asked her mother.

" Who, my girl ? "

" Why, Will ! Will ! Come here, Will, don't run away," she said.

The doctor entered the room, and, after looking carefully at the patient, shook his head.

" Mrs. Thomas," said. he, " I like to be honest at all times.   If she lives to see sunrise to-morrow, she will not see sunset."

The mother broke out into bitter crying and left the room.

That was a strange night at Cefn Ydfa.   The painful screams and the hopeless crying of the young wife, inter-spersed with curses upon her mother and the two Maddocks, and incessant cries for Will Hopkin, made the chamber too dreadful to remain in it.   It was difficult at times to keep her in the bed, for she constantly attempted to rise to meet Will, she said.

" Would that we could get Will here," cried the mother.   " His presence might soothe a little of her tortures.   I would rather than a thousand pounds if I knew where he was ! "

CHAPTER XXVI.

A MONG a party of workmen in the city of Bristol
was one who had a strange peculiarity. He had
been there nearly two years, and not one of his
fellow-workmen had seen a smile on his countenance
during the whole time. During the dinner hour all the
workmen gathered together, but this stranger was
seldom among them. He preferred some lonely corner,
and there his mind wandered to the home of his youth.
His conduct brought upon him the derision of his fellow-
workmen, who called him "Roundhead," a term of
contempt in those days.

However, their conduct had no effect upon him. They
could never rouse his temper. He was never seen out
except when at work.

It is scarcely necessary to intimate that he was Will
Hopkin. During the last week his mind was filled more
than ever with recollections of the Maid of Cefn Ydfa,
and was heard breaking out crying, "Ann! oh, my dear
Ann!" and the tears chased each other down his cheeks.

One afternoon, notwithstanding every effort to prevent
his mind rambling in the direction of the home of his
early life, he was totally unsuccessful. Cefn Ydfa, the
field before the house, with Ann walking therein, played
before his eyes constantly. After finishing his work for
the day he repaired to his lodgings, and was not long
before he went to bed. It was a frightful night in the

beginning of June. The elements were in terrible conflict, the bedroom was lit by lightning, followed the next minute by utter darkness, and the thunder roared until the heavens trembled, and the house shook like a cradle by the force of the storm.

Will Hopkin lay on his bed without taking much notice of the storm, turning uneasily from side to side. He was awake throughout the night until just before the break of dawn, when he fell asleep unconsciously and found himself in the land of dreams. He was walking over a narrow path, well known to him, which led from the village of Llangynwyd to Cefn Ydfa. He imagined that he was going in the direction of the house, and as he surmounted a high stile, which had hidden the house from his sight, he was much frightened at seeing the blinds drawn, as this in Glamorgan signifies that one of the members of the family is dead He stood leaning on the stile, discussing with himself who might be dead. Perhaps it was Mrs. Thomas, or Anthony Maddock, or one of the servants, or it might be his dear Ann was dead ! Whilst thus musing he saw a man coming from the house and walking in his direction. He watched the stranger until he came close enough, when he asked him—

" Who is dead at Cefn Ydfa ? "

" The master of the house," was the answer.

" Master of the house ?" asked Will in surprise. " Has Mrs. Thomas married a second time ? "

" No. Ann's husband—the daughter it was."

" Mr. Maddock, son of William Maddock, the lawyer, of Cwmyrisgla ? "

" Yes, that is the man."

" When did he die ? "

" Late yesterday afternoon."

" What was the cause of his death ? Was he long ill or did he die suddenly ? "

" He fell from his horse last week while hunting, and received injuries which proved fatal."

" The young wife will feel sorry after the husband of her youth, so soon after the marriage ? "

" No, it appears not. It is quietly whispered that she is glad the accident happened, and had informed some of her friends that she hoped it would prove fatal, for she was forced to marry him against her will."

" Did she care for anyone else then ? "

" Oh, yes, Will Hopkin, the thatcher. But he was poor, and her mother discovered that they were courting, and gave orders that he was not to come near the house. But, my young friend, I must go. I am a carpenter, and have been taking the measure of the corpse in order to make the coffin, so I wish you ' Good morning,' " and off he went.

Will remained where he was until the carpenter was out of sight. He could not make up his mind what to do, whether he would go so far as the house or return. At last he resolved to go towards the house. As he entered the yard whom should he see coming out of the house but his beloved Ann. She knew him and ran towards him, and soon was in his embrace. But what a serious change had taken place in her. Instead of the bright girl of eighteen, with spring beauty dancing on her cheeks, she looked sad and heartworn, her cheeks furrowed with pain and trouble, and instead of the ringlets which had hung in beautiful disorder over her shoulders her hair was gathered carefully behind her head, an occasional silver streak being perceptible here and there. But, notwithstanding, the thatcher felt his affection for her as strong as ever, and he kissed her warmly, and felt himself a happy man once again. But—lo ! he awoke, and discovered that all was a dream !

The storm had abated by this time, and the morning sun threw its cheerful rays through the window, filling the bedroom. Will remained for a time in his bed, considering what he had seen and heard in the land of dreams. Was Anthony Maddock really dead ? The question quite confused him. If true, he would return to Llangynwyd at once, and he resolved at last to return to the place of his birth without delay. He did not go to work that morning as usual, and about mid-day his master was much surprised to see Will coming towards him in his best clothes and asking permission to leave. The master did not appear willing, and he did his best to persuade him to remain, but to no purpose. At last permission was given, with a promise that, if ever he asked for work there he should have it. That afternoon Will turned his back upon the city, with his face directed towards Wales.

CHAPTER XXVII.

DEATH OF THE MAID OF CEFN YDFA.

IT was a cloudy and misty day. The rays of the sun did not cheer the meadows, and were it not that its influence was perceptible one might infer that it had not arisen. The wind held its breath, so that there was no breeze whatever. A sad silence reigned over the world.

In a room in Cefn Ydfa lay Ann Maddock in the throes of death. In the intervals between the fits her fearful cries and curses upon her mother for compeling her to marry a man whom she disliked were enough to pierce the human heart.

" My mother, my mother—if worthy of the name— you have sacrificed the happiness of your only child on the altar of your cursed ambition ! You are nothing better than a murderess ! Get out of my sight—far enough ! Where is Will, my dear Will ? Why does he not come ? "

A deep sigh from the breast of her mother saw the only answer. This was followed by painful silence for a time, when Ann broke forth again in wild crying, and saying-

" Mother, come here, and take this hateful ring from my finger. My finger is burning to a cinder, and my heart is a flaming fire ! Off with the ring ! Let me die a free maiden—without the sign of the murderous action, from the effects of which I am now dying, being worn by me. Will ! Will ! my heart, my life ! " She screamed with incredible strength, and then sank upon one of the pillows that supported her.

" Oh, that I knew where Will was that I might send for him ! His presence might lessen a little the torments of my dying child," moaned the mother.

There was no one in the room when these words were spoken, but one of the servants entered soon after, and said that Will Hopkin had just returned home.

" Send for him at once," was her order, and one of the servants was despatched immediately.

Some time afterwards Mrs. Thomas asked, as she lifted her head from a swoon into which she had fallen—

" Has Will come ? "

" Yes," was the answer, " and he has been here some time waiting your permission to enter the room."

" Let him come in at once," she cried, rushing out to ask him herself. In a moment or two she returned accompanied by Will, and, pointing silently to the bed upon which Ann was lying, retired to the next room, giving way to bitter crying.

Some time passed before the Maid of Cefn Ydfa recognised or even took notice of Will, but as soon as she saw and recognised him she attempted to get out of bed towards him, but he stepped forward and prevented her

" Will ! Will ! my dear Will," she cried out in that
unnatural voice which always precedes death. " I love
you always, Will ! You, and you only, are the chief
object of my affections, although I have been forced
to marry another. You are the darling of my soul !
But they have killed me—have shortened my days !
My mother has been a party with our enemies to murder her child ! But I can die peaceably now that I have
seen you and told you that my affections never swerve
from you at all."

Will said nothing, but his swollen breast was ready
to burst with grief, and his eyes were full of tears.

" And this is death ! After a life of trouble and
affliction I am about reaching the long and sweet rest.
I have no fear."

A heavy sigh was the only response.

" Poor Will, my first and only love ! I am glad that
you are here ! I shall die happier now ! It is sweet to
spend the last moments of my life in your company ! "

She stretched her hand towards him, and Will clasped
it in his and bent his head upon it, but grief choked his
utterance, and there was silence for a moment.

" Will," said Ann a second time, " I have one favour
to ask of you. Will you do it ? "

" Anything, my dearest Ann, that you wish."

" Then," said she, extending her left hand towards
him, " take that ring from my finger that I may die a free
maiden in your arms ! It was never mine. You
only I loved, and my murderer's badge shall not be on
my finger in the grave, Will. I would have no rest
even there if it was kept on."

Will hesitated for a minute—did not know what to

do. But she earnestly begged him again, that her body may have rest in the grave, to remove it.

With trembling fingers Will took her hand and removed the ring.

" Keep it, Will, and do not part with it on any account, and remember the unfortunate owner of the finger that was chained to it when she will be mouldering in the grave ! Keep in your memory the Maid of Cefn Ydfa, and her unceasing affection for you in the face of everything, and the cruel means by which she was made a sacrifice to the ambition of her unnatural mother, when she is sleeping in the silent valley. The end is near, Will. I feel the hoar frost of the misty banks of Jordan falling in showers over me, and the dread of the grave is creeping over me."

She closed her eyes, and a great and evident change was coming over her.

" I am afraid—it is so dark," she whispered.

Will saw that the end was close at hand, and went for her mother.

" Come," said he, " she is calling for you."

She rose but her limbs failed to assist her. Will saw she was falling, and supported her to the room.

Ann was leaning on the pillow, and her breathing was difficult. She opened her eyes, beaming with joyful brightness, when she saw Will approaching the bedside.

" My mother," she said, " I forgive you. I am happy—so happy ! Will ! oh, Will ! remember me."

There was a world of tenderness in her eyes and voice, and the tears of Will Hopkin rolled freely as he bent over the bed, pressing his beloved to his breast. She rested her head upon his arm and gazed into his face. The lips which he had often kissed separated, and a heavenly smile passed over her face, and the soul that had suffered was—free !

She rested her head upon his arm and gazed into his face.

PAGE 158.

CHAPTER XXVIII.

THREE days after the death of the Maid of Cefn Ydfa, her mortal remains were laid within the walls of the ancient church of Llangynwyd. Sadly Will Hopkin stood on the brink of the new grave with his eyes fixed upon the coffin which contained the remains of his beloved. "She is no more, she is no more," he murmured, as the earth dropped into the grave and covered the coffin from his sight. There lay, silent and cold, the object in which he had centred all his hopes and comfort—the only woman he had ever loved. The world appeared to him like a vast wilderness. When he lifted his eyes to the blue cloudless sky he thought he heard her voice calling " Oh, my Will, my dearest Will, don't give way to grief after me. My condition to-day is too high for wicked people to cause me any pain ! Remember the happy days we spent together—when our feelings were stimulated in the early mornings by observing Nature unfolding her spring beauties—when we looked at the surrounding hills gilded with the rays of the rising sun and when he illumined the forest with his brightness—the strange feelings that possessed us when walking through the meadows in the gleam of the setting sun ! I am happy and no one could describe the unalloyed, pure and everlasting happiness I now enjoy ! Be strong under your sad fate, and don't give way. Remember that that would increase the joy and happiness of your Ann !

Remember, Will, although the body of your Ann is mouldering in the grave, that her affection for you is without end, and, like her soul, immortal ! "

Nothing could remove the grief of the unfortunate Will Hopkin. She who had gone beyond recall was in him mind constantly. He could not bear the idea of remaining at Llangynwyd, and he soon left the place.

As time passed on, the old village of Llangynwyd remained the same, but great changes took place in the residents, proving the truth of the divine word that our world destroys its inhabitants. Mrs. Thomas, of Cefn Ydfa, was troubled night and day with a guilty conscience, which constantly accused her of having caused the early death of her daughter, and she became towards the end of her days insane. William Maddock managed her affairs, and placed her in an asylum, where she endured the pangs of a guilty conscience, and where she ended her days. After her death the estate of Cefn Ydfa became vested in Anthony Maddock, who resided in the old place. Anthony married a second time within a year of the death of the Maid of Cefn Ydfa.

No one had seen Will Hopkin since the day of the funeral of the unfortunate Ann, and no one knew where he was, or if alive ; and the recollections of him were fast disappearing.

One quiet and cloudy day in August, 1741, fourteen years after the death of the Maid of Cefn Ydfa, a wanderer might have been seen entering the burying ground of Llangynwyd Church, who seemed to take much interest in the inscriptions on the tombstones. The door of the church happened to be open, and he went inside, and proceeded to the chancel, where he stood opposite a stone memorial on the wall, which had carved upon it the following :—

"Here also rest the remains of Ann Maddock, wife of Anthony Maddock, gentleman, of this parish, who died June 16th, 1727."

After reading the inscription, he cried sadly, "Oh, the grave of my dear, dear Ann! Here it is."

It was Will Hopkin, but much altered from what he was when he was last seen in the district! His pale careworn face and tired eyes spoke clearly to the most careless observer of intense mental suffering. After leaving the sacred building, he went in search of work to a farmhouse near by, and was employed to repair the roof of a house, but upon ascending the ladder, his foot slipped, and the poor fellow fell to the ground with such force, that he died before medical help arrived. When preparing the body for burial, a gold ring was found suspended by a string from his neck, the one he had from the Maid of Cefn Ydfa on the day of her death.

His remains were buried under the shadow of a wide-branching yew tree that stood in the churchyard, and in the same grave as his father. A stone was placed to point out the spot where the young bard was laid, but to-day—

> "The rough stone, with its letters crude,
>   By some unskilful friendly hand designed
> In memory of their boyhood days,
>   Lies shattered near with weed entwined."

But if it is lost, his name will remain associated with that of the "Maid of Cefn Ydfa," and his songs to the object of his affections are a sufficient monument to him. Now, the two who loved each other so intensely, and who remained so faithful to each other " until death," unite in their last sleep near each other ; and they will not be awakened until the surrounding hills are gilt with the dawn of the last day, and when sleepers of the dust will be roused by the sound of the trumpet of the archangel from the platform of the cloud !